MIRRORS

JASON YORMARK

DEDICATION

To my two boys, Jacob and Justin, your simple existence is all the inspiration I need to accomplish my goals and aspirations in life. I dedicate my lifelong dream of writing a book to the both of you and hope this inspires you to always chase and accomplish your dreams. I love you both more than you'll ever know!

To my beautiful and amazing wife Molly. Thank you for your support and encouragement in making this book a reality. It doesn't happen without your love and support and for that I am forever grateful. You are the love of my life and inspire me to be more than I ever have. I love you!

To all of my pre-sale supporters, thank you for providing me the kick in the ass I needed to get this book made. Your support will always be incredibly appreciated and a big part of helping make this happen. Thank you!

ACKNOWLEDGMENTS

A big thank you to my first draft feedback team of Dan O'Leary, Kathy Stryker & Kate Mooney. Your early insights helped make MIRRORS even better! Thank you so much!

Big thanks go out to my editor and writing consultant Michael Ruiz. MIRRORS doesn't happen without your incredible insight, edits and assistance in helping make my characters and settings come to life.

Special shout out to my biggest pre-sale supporters, Jeff Kyger, Brian Marchand, Dan Brown, Heidi Millerick, Kristi Toth , Tom Maraday & Tony O'Hanlan. You were the backbone of my pre-sale success. Thank you!

PROLOGUE - 1971

The Manhattan skyline was as warm a hue as the leaves that lined Central Park. Thick bands of orange radiated from beyond the skyscrapers, but no matter how picturesque, the chilling winds that came at night reminded New Yorkers that winter wasn't very far off.

Dale Kerns stood at the crosswalk on 106th and 5th, watching the cars sail past. He could almost feel his wife preparing to comment on how the winds blew curly, grey hairs into his eyes, and how he was past due for a haircut— the sort of near-telepathic intuition that only came from decades of being with one another. But, looking to his right and seeing her own red locks tied back in a tight bun, he knew she was right. Patricia offered him a curt smile before turning her attention to their children.

"Hold Daddy's hand, sweetheart," Patricia said to her son—her Bostonian accent cutting sharply through her words. "The light's about to turn."

Dale watched as Roger paced behind his mother and over to him. He seemed to hold a begrudging hand out to his father, which Dale took without commenting. For a six-year-old, he seemed far too eager to be self-sufficient, and certainly more eager than his twin counterpart Samantha, who stood next to her mother just a few feet away. The light changed, and Dale led his family into the park, making headway straight for the swings.

The park was incredibly vibrant that day. Orange and yellow pierced through the dying leaves, which fell from their trees and lined the sides of the walkways. The winds that caught on the foliage was powerful enough to pull at the piles, sending the leaves over the bounds of the park and bleeding into the concrete city that surrounded them. The beauty of Central Park would soon be lost on Dale—he would only enter the park three more times in his life, and each time would become drearier than the last. The other details of this particular visit would prove to consume any thoughts of his on the trees or the lake.

The pathway forked twice before fading completely away, just as Dale expected. Here, the trees cleared a considerable distance away, leaving a plain field for the playgrounds to occupy. Lining the metal benches along the perimeter were several parents—each watching from afar as their children made fair-weather friends. Dale looked down to his son and daughter, who waited patiently for their cue.

"Stay in the area, alright?" Dale asked of his children. "Make sure you can see me or Mom."

Roger and Sam both ran forward soon afterwards, climbing onto the swings. Dale watched them begin to talk to some of the other children as he and Patricia made for a clear bench. They sat and began to breathe for the first time that day.

"Jesus," Dale sighed, rubbing at his eyes. "We don't get much of a break, do we?"

"They'll understand," Patricia softly replied. She slipped a hand onto Dale's leg. "One day. They'll get it."

Dale smiled. Perhaps he didn't give himself enough of a chance to smile—not before this day, and especially not after. He felt more and more like a cog in the machine of this city. His life before arriving was defined by the rolling plains of upstate New York. After heading to the island to stake his claim, he felt like he had instead traded what was freely his in the first place.

Luckily, Patricia drove such feelings from him. Not only had she been what he found when he came to this city, but she was also a person who felt comfortable in the small life Dale had been able to provide. She was fierce; worked hard to raise Roger and Sam as well as work while they were away at school. And not once did she ever complain.

"You hear from Rob this week?" Dale asked.

Patricia's face seemed to sink for a second into worry, but faded quickly back into her usual vibrancy. "Not yet. I talked to Mom last night and she said not to worry so much. He'd be in the thick of it for the next six months at least."

Something about the words from her raised up his frustration about this particular war. While he was just above the drafting age, Patricia's brother had been far less fortunate. The kids missed Rob's frequent visits to their apartment—his stories of life in the big city always excited them. He made them anxious for the day they'd be out on their own as well.

And now...Rob wasn't.

Somewhere inside Dale, he felt a great shame for being the one in Central Park, and not out there in some Vietnamese trench. The same shame he had felt when his father left when he was a boy. Thoughts like those made Dale wonder about the influence he had upon his son Roger, especially.

While not a single word of this had been spoken between the couple, Patricia seemed to clearly parse the idea from Dale's body language alone. "Hey, relax," she said. "It's okay. He wanted to go, anyway."

"Roger really takes to him," Dale admitted. "And I know it's petty, but sometimes I wonder if I could be a better example over there than out here."

"He'll appreciate the fact that he has a father with him," Patricia said. "And Sam will, too. It's not about being the hero. It's about being here."

Dale looked out to the playground. He could see Roger, grasping at the monkey bars now, high above the ground. His attention couldn't be further away from his parents. Dale watched as he tried hard to skip several rungs, much to the awe of some of the other children. And for a brief moment, he felt alright again.

"Where's Sam?"

Patricia's voice snapped Dale from his momentary trance. He shook off the immediate guilt for not thinking of Sam and began to scan for his daughter. He could make out several children near the swings, and a few on top of the metal structures and playground sides. But none were Sam.

Dale stood up and straightened out his tie, walking to the left to try and get a better view of things. His vantage point slowly shifted, and he was able to keep a sharp eye on the children. He scanned for Sam's red pea coat—a gift from Patricia last Christmas. But the harder he looked, the more worried he became.

He could see his wife approaching Roger and pulling him down from the monkey bars. The two seemed to talk for a second, before Dale could make out his son pointing a finger towards the tree line.

He crossed the park and met up with Patricia, who was already following their son.

"He said she told him she'd be in the woods," Patricia said, who was nearly marching on the heels of their son. He seemed nonplussed—walking calmly towards where his sister said she'd be.

The family jogged up a small hill. Dale could practically feel the other parent's ire at his back, wondering why the family would venture off in a huff. But the more they walked, the less he cared, and the more he worried.

At the crest of the hill, Dale's eyes darted across the narrow clearing they found themselves upon. As luck would have it, he caught a flicker of red to his left. Standing beside an evergreen tree, he could see Sam about a hundred feet away, facing an unknown figure obscured by the trees. Dale walked for just a second, trying to figure out just what he was looking at. A hesitation remembered for a lifetime.

"Sam!" Patricia called out. The voice echoed down the narrow clearing. Sam's head turned sharply towards her family—her face flat, her pale eyes confused.

She took a single step towards them before two coated arms grabbed her by the shoulders, pulling her out of their line of sight.

This time, Dale didn't hesitate. He burst forward as fast as his legs could pull him, but even so, Patricia began to outpace him. It was several long seconds before Dale could round the tree where Sam had been standing.

On the other side, Dale could clearly see a concrete path directly towards the road. And following down it, he found himself next to his wife, staring into the busy city streets, searching for any sign of Sam.

He and his wife screamed out their daughter's name more times than they could count. They shouted so loudly and fervently, a park ranger arrived in minutes. Patricia was the one to explain to the ranger what had happened, while Dale strode up and down the edge of the park, searching from the trees to the road, and back once more to the trees. And in that chaos, Roger was little more than another pedestrian. Another face that wasn't his daughter.

"Dad!" A voice called out.

And for a split second, he thought it was Sam. He jerked back from his position to look towards the sound of the voice.

But standing ten feet from him, shocked and tear-stricken, was his son. "Dad," Roger repeated, ever-quieter.

Dale rushed to his son and embraced him. His face was filling with the same hot tears. His wife, steps away, arguing with a park ranger. It was a moment in time that would last far longer in the memory of those so unlucky to experience it. And Dale nearly begged for the moment to end. That the past few minutes had all been some cruel dream. That somewhere, just among the trees, his daughter would call out for him.

But it wasn't a dream. And he would never hear his daughter's voice again.

2

Blake knocked thrice on the old wooden door.

He kept his stance sharp and cold. This was the Bronx, and no matter how many times he had been here before, no amount of familiarity could ever shake the decades of paranoia he held to. He tried not to look too hard at the three faces several yards down the hall, waiting for an elevator—instead, he kept his gaze low. He raised it only after the door had opened to reveal Dustin, peering out carefully into the halls, and to him.

"Blake," Dustin said, his voice flat and transparent. "You alright?"

"Fine," he responded in kind. "Can we talk for a second?"

The second stretched into several minutes as Dustin allowed Blake into his home and offered him a drink. Blake tried hard to appear as comfortable as he could in the old apartment. Such things were far easier when each wall didn't remind him of the things they had seen.

Blake could tell his friend was surprised at his appearance. Dustin hadn't been around Blake in years, and was no doubt shocked at how much had changed. Blake had to try hard not to scratch at his unshaven face—the nagging feeling of needing a clean shave just another reminder of who he was in the presence of.

"Christ, I haven't seen you since the last time we got the band back together," Dustin said, lying through his teeth. The truth was, the last time Blake had seen him was the funeral. "You keep up with the others?"

"Not usually," Blake said. His hands wrapped around his drink. "They're busier than you."

Dustin took the hint. "Look," he started, "I know it's been too long. I won't bullshit you on that one. It's easy to sink into helping with the Reserve. I'm there probably every hour I'm not home. But I should have called, and I'm sorry."

"I get it," Blake said. His time wasn't going to be wasted on hollow apologies.

"So," Dustin said, forcing a smile, "You ever going to re-involve yourself? I've got a guy below my office in Veteran's Affairs. I told him to look for you if you ever came by, he's got a good offer for a relocation and he needs good men like yourself."

"I've been out for five years," Blake admitted. "And I'm not going to act like those years have been easy, but they've been my choice. I've paid my dues and served my time." He took a swig of beer before continuing: "It's been quiet for sure."

A long pause filled the room—not something these men weren't used to. Blake could fondly remember the long flights and drives over endless desert plains the two had been on not too long ago. There had always been this idea that military men shared this loud, boisterous camaraderie between them. And while that was true is many cases, some of Blake's favorite memories of his tenure were the long, quiet convoy rides across the Arabian Desert.

But this wasn't that sort of silence. Blake wanted something from Dustin, and he had never been good at hiding things from his squad mates. You spend enough time dealing with the shit they'd been through, and you learn to read each other from across far more dangerous territory than the Bronx. Blake decided not to work around his request and took in a deep breath.

"I need your help."

Dustin leaned back in his chair. "Look, Blake, if this is about Casey—"

"Please," Blake interrupted. "I'm not asking much. Just a rudimentary background check on this one guy—"

"Ask the NYPD."

"I don't know anyone in the NYPD," Blake said. "You do."

Blake watched Dustin as he stood from his seat and finished the last of the beer. He moved for the kitchen and opened another before continuing: "I hate to be the guy to say it. I really do, but goddamn—you need to let this go."

"Dustin, just this once."

"Two years," Dustin said, sitting back down. "And I'm sure those have been some of the worst years of your life. Believe me, I couldn't even imagine. But at some point, you're going to have to start healing, and you're never going to do that by keeping up this search."

Blake had expected Dustin not to be as helpful as he once was. Years ago, the first time Blake had asked Dustin a favor concerning his investigation, he was hesitant but ultimately helped Blake find a few sites on the dark net to start searching around. Out of all of the old squad, Dustin was the closest to Blake.

Still, it hurt to hear. "I understand you think I'm crazy for still searching for her," Blake said. "But you have to understand you're not looking at the that data I am. All I'm asking for is a simple background check on one forum moderator."

"You're still on the forums?" Dustin cut in, visibly shocked.

"—just one guy. I've done all I can on my end but I don't have access to these records. If I can back up what he says with what he's done, I might be able to put together some truth to this."

"What happened to you, man?" Dustin said. His face seemed to drop, saying words Blake never expected to hear. "You used to call out anyone for trusting gut feelings, or acting on impulse. Now you're acting like a zodiac sign reading is gonna get you closer to Casey. She was the best thing to happen to you, and I know you don't want to let that go. But you're getting obsessed with—with dark net forums and street rumors, and all of this other shit that's never going to change what happened."

This time, Blake stood up. "I'm not getting lectured at. If you're not interested in doing this for me, that's fine." He set the beer on the table in the center of the room and made for the door. He stopped himself at the handle, turning back around. "I'm not acting on hearsay, Dustin. I'm doing what I've always done. I'm gathering the facts and accessing all possible options." He turned back to the door, his head lowering. "And I am going to find her."

Blake stepped out into the hallway, heading towards the elevators. He got another fifteen feet before he heard Dustin's door open.

"Blake!" Dustin shouted, his voice reverberating down the hallway.

Blake turned in position and looked back at him.

"What's the guy's name?"

"Roger," Blake called back. "Roger Kerns."

Dustin nodded, before turning back to his apartment and latching the door shut.

***

It was an hour and fifteen-minute commute from Dustin's apartment in the Bronx to Blake's studio in Queens. One train and two busses later, Blake found himself climbing familiar stairs to the third floor. He undid the lock and deadbolt, and stepped inside.

Blake's studio was far more of a workspace than any sort of living quarter. He had been renting it out for somewhere over a year now, and enjoyed the seclusion it provided from the otherwise busy streets. His neighbors were quiet, his landlord even quieter, and the isolation proved far fitting for the line of work Blake had committed to.

He stepped into the kitchen and quickly brought a pot of water to boil. He dumped dry noodles inside before moving into the main studio space. To his left and right, maps of New York lined the walls. Some of the island entirely, but others of smaller sections—districts and boroughs he had been keeping an eye on ever since. He had his computer half-buried in papers and folders on the left-hand side, and further information and dirty clothes continued down the wall from there.

On the right, his sofa sat, wading in a sea of journals and folders. It was all a part of a strange organization process of his—keeping the most important ideas closest to the computer. The far less reasonable ideas stayed by the sofa, for Blake to look at during dinner and lunch breaks. Interestingly enough, the idea to search for Roger had come from the sofa—not the computer.

In the far back corner of the room was where Blake would spend his nights. Old bedsheets lined a lumpy mattress that desperately needed replacing. It had been so easy to fall back into old habits, even after all this time. It seemed not even the military could break habitual messiness. Only Casey was able to do that.

Blake sat himself at the computer and lifted his hands to the keys. The old thing sputtered back on, pulling up the dozens of tabs and windows he had left open—each with a specific task in mind. He moved quickly to a familiar site to see if Roger was online. Next to his username, a small circle glowed red. Blake wasn't too surprised; even though he had discovered Roger had lived in New York his whole life, the time was still well past two in the morning, and Roger seemed to get off for the night around eleven.

For the past three months, Blake had been pulling every string he could to de-mask this anonymous source. From relentlessly searching through old forum posts and tracking his habits to determine a time zone, to even pressing other users on the site for any sort of hint or indication of his name. None of his efforts were in vain. If the things Roger claimed were true, it could be the break that Blake had been waiting for. The one he so desperately needed, especially now.

Today was the two-year anniversary of the day Casey was taken. And each night that passed lowered the chance that Blake would ever see his wife again.

3

Central Park was a perfect place to arrange a meeting. It had taken quite a bit of convincing, but Roger had ultimately agreed to a spot near Wien Walk, in plain view of the patrolling law enforcement, as well as the general public—Wien Walk was one of the busiest spots in the city.

Three days prior to their meeting, Blake had gone ahead and scouted out the exact location that would work best for them. From watching what the typical routes were for the patrolling officers, to any sort of escape route he would need to take, Blake had studied and prepared as much as he could for this day.

It wasn't for distrust of Kerns, however. Roger seemed like an average person, albeit rather timid. It was the principal of the matter. The basic tenants of his training kicking into gear as he traversed into the more obscure reaches of the world. After all, he had arranged a meeting over the dark net. Perhaps some justified paranoia would be best for the situation.

So for now, Blake entered Wien Walk and trailed a few local patrons. The pathway here was wide and the diversity of the people provided ample cover for him. Blake pulled at his ball cap and took a glance just past the corner, towards the agreed-upon spot.

Roger wasn't there—and he was several minutes late.

Blake turned left at the corner and circled back around towards an alternative route. Out here, the especially windy day was blowing leaves out of the trees, littering the edges of the park in green. Blake saw this pragmatically. The more of an opportunity for distraction and cover, the better.

But what was he doing? He couldn't shake the thought. His response to Casey's disappearance had been logical; almost assumed. His search had taken years, sure, but it had mostly been within piles of work, and within his own apartment. This was field work—something that came easily to Blake, but in all of the wrong ways. More and more these days Blake felt less like a civilian and more like a soldier; invading a foreign land, searching for his target by any means necessary.

It was all true, but for different reasons. Blake's search for Casey wasn't fueled in the same way his searches in the past had been. Those had been for duty, for country, but mostly because he had been damn good at it. No, this was a search for his life. The life he had earned after so many years in war. The life he had finally began to get comfortable within. Casey had shown him what it was like to be a civilian again. Through her, he had learned to finally embrace normal.

Now, with each passing day, he was treating the search for her with more and more cold duty. And it was beginning to scare him, but he knew no other way to find her. Not without losing himself entirely.

The second time around Wien Walk, Blake made sure to stop at a street salesman, picking up a hotdog. He sloppily ate half of it before coming back into the line of sight of the location.

And there he was.

Roger sat uneasily on a small corner of the park bench Blake had referenced to him. His shoulders were high and tense—his eyes darted from person to person in his immediate vicinity, but no further. His skin was splotchy and greasy, no doubt from lack of hygiene. He seemed uncomfortable in his own body, and held his arms close to his beer belly. He couldn't be any more nervous than a teenager at his first drug deal. Yet, he could hold the key to Blake finding himself again.

Blake tossed the rest of the food into the trash and started walking wide, watching for anyone with a visual on Roger. Three stood out to him: a father with his son, who seemed to be looking for a place to sit, a park ranger, and a woman. From the three of them, she seemed the most suspicious; in the hot summer day, she had chosen an exceptionally nice dress to wear. And, at two in the afternoon, it was far too early to justify her going to an event. He made a mental note to keep a keen eye as he approached.

"You need to calm down," Blake said, short as he sat comfortably beside Roger. He could feel Roger jump in his seat at the sound of him, physically jolting and looking right at him.

"Blake?" Roger said. His voice was as shaky as the rest of him.

"Relax your shoulders," Blake continued. "Turn your body towards me. We're two friends having a conversation."

Roger seemed to attempt a more natural posture, but fell flat. "You think we're being watched?"

"You're going to need to calm down," Blake repeated. "And you're going to need to start talking."

Roger blinked rapidly. He looked down, back towards the main path, over to the trees, and finally made eye contact. "I talk, you talk. Th-that's the deal, right?"

Blake nodded.

"Okay, look," Roger said. "What I told you over the forums is what I know. People go missing all of the time around here."

"Then why are we meeting?" Blake countered.

"Because they all go to the same place," Roger explained. "They have to. I've been keeping up with police reports for years now. If any man, woman, or child—especially child—goes missing in the state of New York, I log it. I look into the locations, I check them out, ask around—I do whatever I have to. A lot of these are what you would expect. Kidnappings, violent and sexual assaults, you name it. But some stand out."

Roger seemed to loosen as he talked. Blake could read eyes very well, and Roger's seemed to light up in a way no liar's ever could. So far, so good.

"All of these missing persons reports have motives," Roger continued. "Revenge stories, lust, shame, all of the usual things you would hear about on the news. Nothing exciting. Even the cases that go unsolved have clearer answers than they'd like to lead you to believe. But I've noticed a pattern."

As Roger continued on, Blake couldn't help but continue to keep a close eye on the three people that had a close visual on their conversation. The park ranger had slipped away, and the father as well, but the woman in the dress seemed to keep within eyeshot. From his periphery, he could make her form out behind Roger's head—her body leaned against a nearby tree.

She was looking directly at them.

"Stand up with me," Blake said, cutting Roger off. Blake stood and took a few steps from the bench, waiting for Roger to follow suit.

"Walk with me," Blake said.

"Why—"

"We're going to make a short perimeter around the park," Blake continued. As the two walked away, he didn't bother to continue looking for the well-dressed woman.

"I talk, you talk, remember?" Roger asked. His voice was beginning to raise too loud for Blake's comfort. "That was the deal."

"We were being watched," Blake said, responding automatically. The rest of him was scanning the route forward, ensuring their safety. "Who did you tell about this?"

"What? No one," Roger defended. "Why would I have?"

"Around here," Blake said. He slipped into a nearby play area and into the tree line—off from the main path. Once he felt out of the view of the general public, he turned back to Roger: "Because there's no other reason for us to be followed right now."

"Jesus Christ," Roger said under his breath. "There's no reason someone would be looking for you, is there?"

Blake's face went cold. "What about you?"

Neither man spoke at the impasse.

Finally, Blake broke the silence: "You were talking about a pattern."

"Look, it's circumstantial at best," Roger started, "but it's a start. Some of these missing reports have similar variables. Reports with no motives, no family history of crime, nothing to allude to what happened to them. But most damning of all is what happens after someone goes missing."

"What do you mean"

"Some of these cases involve large disbursements to the family," Roger said. "Sometimes it looks like a settlement deal, other times like unemployment benefits or assisted living programs. Other cases result in strange relocations. Entire families that have never left New York for generations, all ending up in foreign countries around the world. And some even involve more missing people, more freak accidents."

"You're implying some sort of grand conspiracy," Blake said. "You know that, right? You're saying bureaucracy is covering something up. Bureaucracy is going to far as to *kill people.*"

"I know it sounds crazy, but I've talked with some of these families," Roger continued. "They're dismissive. Avoidant. Even if I'm trying to help them with possibly reopening the cases of their missing person, they start threatening to call the cops."

"How do you know so much about this?" Blake asked. His mind was racing with possibilities.

"Because," Roger said. "It happened to me, too."

Everything Roger was saying seemed plausible. From the information Dustin had gathered, to the clear body language he was showing, Blake had little reason to doubt him. Sure, he sounded insane. But the only two options were that he was either insane, or telling the truth.

And given the things Blake had known and seen, it didn't seem too far-fetched.

Behind Roger, Blake could see a flash of a red dress. His eyes lifted to see the woman from earlier, near the bench—she walked carefully on the cobblestone path, scanning the faces of each person as they walked by. Anyone with a keen eye could see she was an anomaly in this park; a person with a far more sinister reason for being here than most.

"She's there," Blake said aloud. Roger turned and looked in his direction, seeing her. Luckily, both of them were out of her field of vision—obscured by the trees around them.

"Who?"

"Wait here," Blake said. His instincts propelled him into motion, and he stepped out onto the main pathway behind her.

"Blake!" he heard Roger call out from behind him. His voice drowned in the sea of chatter out here.

Hearing the noise, the woman in the red dress turned in place. Her brown hair floated and whipped behind her, and immediately locked eyes with Blake, who was standing just three feet behind him.

Her face froze. This close to her, Blake was able to scan every feature. The sharpness of her cheekbones. The way her auburn hair curled and frayed. The hue of her eyes. Anything and everything he could need to recognize her should he loose her again.

"Hi," Blake said, smiling. "I'm going to need you to tell me why you're following us."

"I'm not sure what you mean," she replied. Her voice rang indignant.

"Then why'd you turn around when you heard my name?"

Her demeanor changed as Blake spoke. Her face dropped into a morose glare. She looked him up and down, for just a second.

Then, she ran.

Blake's body moved before his mind. He sprinted after her. Patrons of the park from the left and the right both jumped out of the way. Somewhere far behind Blake, he thought he heard Roger call out his name.

The two sliced past the main pathway as the woman in the red dress ran into an open field. Blake's vision focused solely on his target, and any other sounds or distractions quickly faded away. His only thought process was his breathing, his speed, and his stamina.

And he was quickly closing in on her.

It was about another ten seconds before Blake leapt forward, grabbing the woman by the shoulders and sending them both onto the ground. Blades of grass covered Blake as he rolled twice past her, then quickly got up and pinned her to the ground.

"Please," she stammered. She panted, trying to catch her breath. "You're making a mistake."

"You need to *start talking.*" Blake said. "*Now.*"

Before another word could be said, Blake felt a large force to his left, and soon enough, it was him that was tackled to the ground.

The park rangers had finally intervened.

4

"I could charge you with disturbance of the peace," the police officer said, "but assault would probably look better in court. It's your choice, really."

Blake and Roger found themselves sitting across from an NYPD officer in a cold, dark room. It had been several hours since park rangers had detained him, and later Roger, for questioning. After much arguing with the ranchers, they had detained the woman in the red dress as well.

And it was all Blake could think about as the officer gave his standard threatening spiel. Perhaps, if they had known who they were talking to, they would have known it would never work.

"I want to know why I was being followed," Blake said, "And I want to be sure that I know who it was that was following me."

"What about you?" The officer said, his gaze turning now to Roger. "Any reason coming from you?"

Roger, luckily enough for Blake, had immediately known to keep his mouth shut from the moment he entered the police department. Whether that was from prior experience or not remained to be seen, but at least he said nothing about the dark net. Looks like he took Blake's story about being old friends to heart.

"I don't see why we were being followed." Roger said. He kept his eyes locked onto the table. "Blake's incendiary, sure, but that doesn't excuse it."

The police officer sighed, but before he could say another word, the door opened, and another officer stepped in, handing the him a manila folder. The other officer left quickly, and the first scanned the documents in his hands.

"Well, well," the police officer said, "Looks like you were a Marine."

Blake's eyes narrowed. "Still am."

"Hmm," was all the officer said. "You'd think you'd know better than to go around tackling women in parks." The officer next turned to the door, opening it. "But," he continued, "she's not pressing charges. So, it seems like it's your lucky day."

Blake stood from the chair, rushed for the door, and into the main lobby of the police department. Without hesitation, Blake pushed past the other occupants of the building and the double doors of the station to find himself back onto the streets of Manhattan. Since their time inside, the sun had set and the clouds had covered the moonlit sky. The frigid rain struck against Blake as he scanned the faces that walked past. Up and down, up and down, he looked for some sort of answer, or some clue. But it was already too late.

The woman in the red dress had long since left the building.

Never had he felt closer to an answer, and yet so far from one.

"Blake, wait!"

Blake turned around to see Roger head down the steps, holding his hat to his head. "They let her go twenty minutes ago. We're not going to find her."

Blake knew he was right. He had been trained in manhunts before. The possibility of finding one woman in a city as large as this was beyond laughable. But the statistics didn't make the loss hurt any less.

"What now?" Roger asked.

Blake looked at him through the rain, and for a moment, wasn't sure what to say. "I don't know," he said after a long pause. He turned towards the subway station. "I don't think I can help you."

"W-wait! Hold on!" Roger called out. Blake felt his hand get pulled, and turned back towards the man. "I talk, you talk. I told you what I know."

"I don't have anything to give you," Blake said calmly. "I'm sorry."

And yet Roger was persistent. "You're ex-military, right?" He asked. "Look; I know you think I'm crazy. I get it. But we just got trailed for a damn good reason, and I want to know what that reason is. There's got to be someone you can talk to about this. I dunno—maybe an old co-worker, or a friend. You have to have contacts."

"You don't think I haven't already done that?" Blake said. He could feel his voice getting louder. More and more, the stress of being so close was starting to come out of him. "You don't think I haven't already tried talking to *everyone*?"

Roger looked down to the floor, then back up. "It was your wife, wasn't it? She's the one that went missing?"

Blake paused for a moment, before realizing he had never told Roger, on the internet or otherwise, his reasons for investigating. "Two years ago. Almost to the date."

"I've been looking for decades," Roger said. "And there's more people out there, I know it." Roger dug around in his pockets and produced a card. He pulled out a pen and scrawled several numbers down onto it. "Look, just call me if something comes up. I'm never that far off."

And with that, Roger disappeared into the Friday evening crowds, leaving Blake alone on the streets, in one of the busiest cities in the world.

Where the hell did that woman go?

***

Elsewhere in the city, Dustin was locking the door behind him at his Bronx apartment. Today had been another particularly long and stressful day—the physical toll of field work had long since replaced itself with the mental agony of office work. Being stationed back at home permanently was surprisingly one the most depressing parts of the career.

Still, it was nice to have a change of pace. Being in the shit for so long, you eventually develop a complex for being back home, and on the days Dustin enjoyed it, he *really* enjoyed it.

It was a Friday night, and the last thing Dustin wanted to do was get out of the house. He moved to his fridge and pulled out a beer, before collapsing haphazardly onto his couch. He had just wrapped his fingers around the television remote when his work cell phone rang violently in his pocket. After another two rings, he had fumbled with it enough to raise it to his ear.

"Hello?"

"Sergeant Barnes," came an all-too-familiar voice. "Good to hear from you."

Any sort of calm evening dissipated immediately when Dustin heard the voice on the other end of the line. The number was always different, the circumstances always changed, but anytime *she* called, it was always a sign of trouble. "What is it?"

"It's your friend," the voice said. "Blake Collier. Have you seen him recently?'

"He stopped by the other day," Dustin said. He kept his tone even and straight. "Asked for a favor."

"Which you granted by running an illegal background check on a military network, is that right?"

"He's an old friend." Dustin said. He had given up on any sort of defense.

"You were *supposed* to get him to talk to our contact about relocation," she said.

"I'm not in the business of forcing my friends into meetings," he replied. "I mentioned it. he's not interested."

"Well," the voice continued, speaking in her usual cool cadence. "I'm not in the business of telling you who or who not to be in contact with. But I'll need a favor from you."

"And what might that be?"

"The next time Blake Collier decides to show up at your doorstep, you lock your door. You don't let him in, and you *certainly* don't pull any more 'favors' for him, either."

"With all due respect, ma'am," Dustin started. "Ignoring Blake will only make things worse. You don't know him. Anytime he feels pushback, he just goes after what he wants harder."

"Oh, Barnes," the voice said. Dustin could hear the contempt in her voice. "Have you forgotten everything we've done for you? The things we've let slide, the cushy desk job we've given to you?"

"Of course not," Dustin said.

"Then maybe show a little more *appreciation* next time we ask you to do the smallest of favors."

Dustin took a deep breath. "What's he doing that's so dangerous?" He dared to ask.

"Let's just say, he's barking up the wrong tree, and leave it at that. But your assistance to Blake in any capacity is over. Understood?"

"Yes ma'am." He sighed. Even after years of this, Dustin had never even learned the woman's rank.

"Good." The voice said, and the line went dead soon after. After a moment to be sure, Dustin tossed the phone to the floor. Hard.

Lying to Blake for years was hard enough, and the years of blackmail weren't making it any easier.

Dustin moved to turn the television on and left it on the first channel that appeared on the screen. He turned it loud enough to drown out his own thoughts, and closed his eyes.

Why couldn't Blake just let it die with her?

5

It had been three days since Blake first met Roger in Central Park. And in those three days, he had accomplished nothing. It was only after three days that Blake had decided to swallow his pride and call him. He was about to board the morning subway train, and the phone rang hardly once before he could hear Roger pick up the phone.

"Hey," Roger said through the receiver. His voice already seemed to have an idea of who was calling.

"It's Blake. You have some time this evening to touch base?" Blake asked. He looked around at the other faces around him, almost ashamed. "I can swing by and maybe look at what you've got."

"She's stuck in your head, isn't she?" Roger said. And for a moment, Blake wasn't sure if Roger was referring to Casey, the woman in the red dress, or both.

"Text me your address," Blake said, ignoring his question. The subway doors ahead of him had already opened. "I'll swing by this evening."

Blake hung up the phone without waiting for a response and entered the subway bus. On a good day, he normally sensed the strange paranoia of feeling watched.

After meeting Roger in Central Park, every day seemed to be a sea of eyes, staring down at him.

He could only hope today's meeting would be fruitful.

Blake had decided to move back to Dustin with some of the new information. And if he was being honest, throughout the journey to the apartment, he wasn't sure what to say. Dustin was a sort of last bastion to Blake—one of the few people he felt comfortable enough around to talk to, even if it had been years since he and Dustin had really had an honest conversation with each other. As he approached the doorway, Blake thought of the war:

He and Dustin were two of the highest ranking officers in his group. They—along with Jordan, another officer—led their squad through the slums of the Arabian cities, and the quiet beauty of the deserts that surrounded them. It was on one of these dunes outside their camp that he and Dustin had really spoken last. Blake had a falling out with Jordan at the time and needed an ear to listen. He told Dustin all about the woman he had met out there, and the worries he had about returning to civilian life.

"I don't know if I can be what she needs," Blake had said to Dustin. "I don't know if I can be that kind of man anymore."

"Mate," Dustin had joked. "She's already picked you. You're already what she wants you to be."

Out there, the bullshit of the cities and the comfort fades away. The only thing that remains, is what you really are. And Blake and Dustin were cut from the same cloth. Always had been.

Blake arrived back at Dustin's apartment unannounced, and his memories of the war faded as he knocked on the wooden door.

He had initially thought it could be beneficial just to stop by, but the look on his friend's face as he opened the door was more than enough to signal something was off.

Dustin's gaze had a glaze to it—the same glaze that Blake had noticed in himself from lack of sleep.

"Blake, what is it?" Dustin asked. He didn't move from the doorway.

"I figured I'd just swing by—" Blake managed to get out, before Dustin's hand raised, stopping his speech. The two of them had known each other long enough to know when the other was lying.

"I helped with the background check, but that's it," Dustin said. There was a sharp sense of finality to his voice. "I'm finished helping with this."

"I'm just here to ask if you knew of any sort of investigation or study on missing persons around the city. That's all."

"I've held my tongue about this for long enough," Dustin said. "But it's time for you to drop this."

"I'm pretty sure you said that to me last time."

"No one's questioning your loyalty, Blake," Dustin said. "And it's always good to see you again. Most of us were worried you wouldn't ever recover. But if you're going to constantly berate me about conspiracies and lies, maybe it's best if you stopped coming over."

Blake took a deep breath. "I met Roger in Central Park, and someone was following us. A meeting arranged on a harmless forum on the dark net and we have people watching us. I'm just trying to figure out who the hell would care so much."

"Goodbye, Blake."

Dustin closed the door on Blake, leaving him standing alone in the long hall. In all of the years Blake had known him, Dustin had never acted like that.

He didn't know what, but something was seriously wrong. With Dustin, with Roger, with the woman in the dress...none of it was lining up. The ideas Roger suggested were crazy—unfounded, even. But the idea that people were interested enough to physically track them down was even stranger. And now, with Dustin being completely antagonistic over simple questions? He was going to need to do something. And soon.

***

It was a good twenty seconds after Blake had knocked on Roger's door before it opened, revealing a terrible smell emanating from inside the apartment. Peering from around the edge of the door, Roger seemed to make sure it was Blake before opening it completely.

"Honestly," Roger said. "I didn't think you were going to come."

"Look," Blake started. "This isn't about anything else other than the search. I'm in and out if you don't have anything I think could help me."

"I get it," Roger said. He seemed a bit disappointed. "I'll show you what I've got, then."

Roger stepped aside and allowed Blake inside.

The first thing Blake noticed about the apartment was the clutter of it all. The tables and floors of the place were covered in books and papers like his, but also wrappers, trash, and empty takeout boxes. Moldy plates were stacked in the corner of the room just to the side of the door, and the apartment curved around to the kitchen from here, where a makeshift work station had been carved out from the filth.

"It's shit, I know," Roger said. "You don't have to be nice about it."

"Christ," Blake said under his breath. And Casey thought *he* was messy.

"I'm easily distracted, I guess," Roger continued. "Especially recently. There isn't much other than the investigation that takes up my mental space." Roger led Blake across the room towards the kitchen. "I got the place after my uncle offed himself. I guess Vietnam finally got to him, I don't know. But I get enough from his will and a nice severance package at my old job to keep the lights on."

"What did you use to do?" Blake asked, trying to find a clear place to walk.

"Statistics, mostly," he said. "I got really into numbers and data. It's kind of stemmed from this lifelong search."

The more he talked, the less Blake was interested in hearing him out. He was a train-wreck, certainly, but perhaps the data would be worth dealing with him. "What's all this?" Blake asked, pointing to a wall map coated in thumb tacks.

"This is every reported disappearance in the state of New York," Roger said. There was a hint of triumph in his voice. "Or at least, the important ones, that is. The black tacks are cases marked as open, and the red ones closed with no body found. You'd be surprised how many years they'll act like they're helping a family, only to tell them they've barely found a thing at all."

Blake studied the wall of tacks. "There doesn't seem to be any correlation."

"Exactly," Roger said. "That's the part that always gets me. Nothing about these disappearances make sense. There's no continuity of gender, age, race—any of it. But you see these green tacks?"

Blake looked at the dozen on the map marked green. "Yeah?"

"These are the noteworthy ones. All the same parameters—missing person with no motive to speak of, with either strange changes in income, relocations, or other family members missing or dead. I've been looking into these— twice as hard after we met up. Any discrepancy, any sort of factor I might have missed, I'm writing down."

"That's your plan?" Blake asked. "Look into a couple of case files and see what sticks out?"

"You have any other ideas?" Roger shot back. He looked to Blake for a moment, before sitting down near a stack of papers. "This is all I've got. If you have any sort of ex-military knowledge or resources, you're welcome to tell me. But otherwise, start looking."

Blake stood and thought hard about walking out, right then and there. Taking a major step back and re-assessing the other options. Any other motive or path that could lead to Casey. But no matter how hard he thought, there wasn't a single lead as enigmatic or as promising as this.

"You've got something to drink?" Blake finally asked, moving towards the kitchen.

***

It was four hours later, and Blake had spent most of the evening reading reports on missing persons that lay around Roger's apartment. The different stories all seemed so similar and yet so different—the grand strokes of each missing person the same, with the different little details and nuances of a whole life. It was exhausting to read into and no matter how much Blake focused on the details, he couldn't make any logical conclusions with any of it. He could see now why Roger had been so eccentric before. Blake couldn't imagine decades of a fruitless search like this.

"There's got to be some central location," Roger said after a significantly long period of silence. Blake raised his head and looked to him. "I mean," Roger continued, "if there's some sort of bureaucratic infrastructure to this. Some hub, at least in the state or maybe the region."

"Roger, I've been to every military base and office in New York," Blake said. "None of them have any sort of organization to pull off that sort of operation. Nothing stateside, at least."

"I don't know," Roger said. He lowered his head back into the page he was looking at. "It's all random, sure, but there's got to be a pattern. At one point, I sent a lot of this data to some contacts I met over the forums, like yourself."

"Did they figure anything out?" Blake asked.

Roger shook his head. "Closest I ever got was some guy talking about a spot way off the grid, near a city no one ever goes into. He wouldn't say the name of the place, and he never got back online after we talked about it. Other than that, nothing. Even after I scanned all the satellite imagery of the state, I couldn't find a thing he was talking about."

Blake thought for a second. "My hands are tied here," he admitted. "I work in the field. Always have. Looking through this stuff…well, it just makes me want to blow my damn brains out."

Roger stood up and moved to the kitchen, and quickly produced two more beers. He tossed one of the cans over to Blake, and sat himself back down. "You don't have a way to check records of operations in the state?"

"I was active duty only five years ago," Blake said. "I would have known about a place like that."

"Maybe it was an issue of security," Roger said. "A high enough clearance level to find out about the place."

"You don't have a damn clue how the armed forces work," Blake snapped. "So stop acting like it."

"Christ, fine," Roger conceded, and once again lowered back into the paperwork. "Sorry I asked. Just guessing here."

It was another twenty minutes before either of them spoke again.

"You still talk to those guys?"

Blake rubbed at his temples. *God, what time was it?*

"What guys?" Blake asked.

"Any of the guys you served with," Roger explained. "I mean, there's got to be a few of them around."

"I mean, sure, but I don't talk to them," Blake said. "Like I told you outside the police station, I've tried everything on my end. The only guy that'll talk to me just blew me off."

Roger made a sort of 'uh-huh' noise, and stretched out his back. "So much for sticking together."

"It wasn't always like this," Blake said. "At least not with this one guy. We used to be inseparable before my wife disappeared. He was best man at my wedding and everything. But something's got him acting strange and he's done with helping me in any way."

"When did that start?" Roger asked. "Before or after Central Park?"

Blake didn't respond, but the seed had been planted in his mind. *How much information did Dustin have on this from his end?* It was a crazy thought, but never had Blake entertained the notion that any of his military contacts would know about some sort of conspiracy. Hell, he had only *just* entertained the notion that there was systemic human trafficking to begin with. Most likely, this lead would end in another dead end—the same way as all the leads that had come before it. But something was growing in Blake's mind.

"What were some of the ways you're guessing at here?" Blake asked. "Ways they've been covering their tracks?"

"It's case-by-case," Roger said. "But it's consistently strange. A family in Albany living in poverty suddenly owning the business hotel in town after a father goes missing. A couple in Buffalo relocating to Paris a year after their daughter goes missing. A wealthy businessman with no history of mental illness throwing himself off of the Brooklyn Bridge after his mother vanishes in Queens."

"And you said a guy knows about a hidden base out off the grid?"

"He mentioned it, yeah," Roger said. He seemed rather confused as Blake's sudden interest. "But like you said, it probably doesn't exist, and there's no way for us to check if it does."

The more he talked, the more Blake wondered about Dustin's offer at the V.A about relocation. He had only ever mentioned it after Casey disappeared. Said it came with lucrative deals and a nice cushy gig like his. Blake had always blown him off before, but now the idea was planted in his head. Could Dustin know more than he was letting on?

"Blake, if someone is talking to you," Roger said. "If anyone's trying to get you to accept money, or some far-flung job...you need to look into it."

"So what?" Blake asked. "You receive money?"

"My Mom and Dad moved from the city once I was old enough to stay," Roger continued. "I got some money, for a while, but not much."

"Your own theory doesn't hold well to your own experience. Why do you think they stopped?"

"I'm not a threat to whoever is doing this," Roger said. "You are."

Blake left Roger's place soon after, promising to call him back if he figured out anything else. On the way back, thoughts of Dustin plagued him more and more, and finally, sometime around midnight, he picked up the phone and gave him a call.

"What," Dustin said, answering just before Blake was sent to voicemail.

"I gave it some thought," Blake said, "and I think I'm going to take you up on that offer to meet your guy at V.A. this week."

There was a long pause. "Well, I'm glad to hear it," Dustin said. "It's all in this big complex just north of Port Chester. My office is connected to the whole building."

"I think I remember it," Blake said. "I'll come by in a few days."

"Glad to hear it," Dustin said. His voice seemed cheerier, but dropped low soon after. "Look, about earlier today, I'm sorry if I came across like a dick. I'm just...tired of seeing you stuck in the past."

It took a lot for Blake not to respond with anything more than: "I get it."

Blake hung up the phone with mixed feelings. If there was any way to give legitimacy to Roger's ideas, he was going to have to talk to this man and see what sort of offer he was making. And, if he could, access a computer terminal at the V.A. office and enter the private network. Roger was wrong about rank, but right about one thing; if a base existed in any sort of official capacity, it would be accessible in Dustin's terminal in his office. Even more so if Dustin was presumably in on whatever was going on. It was the last thing Blake even wanted to do, but what choice did he have?

Dustin was hiding something, and the more Blake thought about it, the more damning that thought became.

6

The Office of Veteran's Affairs was a grey brick building just outside of Port Chester.

The building it occupied had clearly been on the path of collapse for a long time, and no amount of internal renovation could like the cracks that ate at the corners, nor the paint that flaked from the decaying walls. And through the clouded windows that lay on the exteriors, Blake could see inside that the building had just recently opened. He had made it a point to arrive early and shave the stubble from his face, and entered the building with as honest a smile as he could muster.

What he was about to do was illegal at best—and treasonous at worst. Gaining access to Dustin's computer files would involve breaking more laws that he could think of. But, if the answers today got him anywhere closer to Casey, it would have all been worth it.

Just inside the building, Blake waited on a bench until Dustin could be called from his office. Not five minutes later, he did arrive—trailed by an older, smiling man, wearing a plain black polo and a veteran cap.

"Glad to see you came," Dustin said, shaking Blake's hand. He motioned next to the man behind him. "This is Peter. He's been with us a long time."

"Good morning, sir," Blake said to the man. The two shook hands.

"Semper Fi," Peter said in response—the traditional greeting.

From there, Dustin led Blake and Peter downstairs, past the cafeteria and towards what looked to be a common break room. As he did so, Blake's eyes were anywhere but in front of him.

Scanning the structure of the building, Blake could tell the V.A office was split into two halves—a first area for the public and other veterans to meet and relax, but also a secondary area. A sea of offices could be seen through the interior windows, above them on the third and fourth floors of the office area. That was where Dustin and the other active service members worked, and the general public was prohibited. It was *also* where Blake could gain access to the military network, check the registries, and find out for certain whether or not any facilities in the state had the infrastructure like the one Roger was talking about.

Dustin excused himself once he got Peter and Blake on some couches in the lounge, leaving to go back to work. Checking his watch, Blake estimated he had about an hour and a half to kill before Dustin would go to lunch.

For the next hour, Blake and Peter talked about anything and everything. It wasn't the fault of Peter that Blake didn't care for the conversation—he seemed like a nice enough man, and the bond between fellow Marines was never something to doubt. However, he was on a mission today, and that couldn't be averted by anyone. The only thing this man could prove to Blake was his suspicion that *someone* was trying to move him away from the scene of the crime.

And Peter's proposal was certainly damning. An offer for a lucrative position in central Florida, near a beach and with housing provided by the state. "A respectable job," as Peter put it, that would involve working as liaison between other departments in the area.

All the while, Blake thought back to the dozens of papers in Roger's apartment, and all of the places other people had been relocated to suddenly after a disappearance. A public defender in a prized New York district moved out to Salt Lake City, a family with three generations within a small Albany suburb suddenly moving to Missoula...the list went on. This would have been yet another addition to Roger's list—a Marine born and bred in New York suddenly moving to Florida without spouse or family. Blake let the man speak, but his words only encouraged him to go through with today's mission.

"Let Dustin know I had to go," Blake said as he stood up from the couch exactly eighty-five minutes after sitting down. He feigned typing out a text message. "I'm sorry about this, really. I completely forgot about the appointment."

"It's alright," Peter said with a smile. He extended a hand out. "It was nice to meet you, Collier. Give me a call when you can."

Blake shook the man's hand and promptly turned to the exit. He stepped outside, rounded the block a single time, and found an excellent vantage point—a coffee shop just outside and across the street from the offices. Blake ordered a large coffee, sat with a paper, and bided his time.

As it had turned out, Blake had estimated Dustin's lunch break almost exactly. Within another two minutes, he could see Dustin and several other officers step outside, laughing as they turned around the block.

Blake had to move, and fast. He tossed the cup away and headed back inside the offices.

He scanned first to see if there were any signs of Peter, but luckily, there were none. Blake paced across the carpet towards the easiest way into the restricted areas.

"Excuse me," Blake said, smiling as bright as he could. He had approached the front counter of the cafeteria. Behind the counter, a middle-aged woman stood—the only person stationed here. She wore typical daytime clothes, save for a bright blue vest that seemed to indicate her position as a cafeteria worker. Just what Blake would need.

"Yes?"

"I was in here earlier, and I think I left my phone somewhere," Blake lied. He pointed a finger towards the lounge. "Just over there. I already checked it out, but I didn't see it over there. You don't think there's a lost and found here, do you?"

"I'm sorry sir," the worker responded. "I don't think we have one."

"I hate to ask, but could you check for me? It'd really mean a lot."

The lady sighed, and turned towards the door Blake had been eyeing the entire time—the door between the two halves of the building. On it, in thick blue ink, it could clearly be read: *Authorized Personnel Only.*

"I can ask security if they picked anything up," she said.

"Thank you, I really appreciate it."

Blake waited until ten seconds passed from when she entered the room, until he moved around the counter. With no one around, he quickly searched the cafeteria. There were stainless steel plates and bins everywhere, but the only corner of the area that showed any sign of color was the far right corner. Blake quickly approached and found exactly what he had been looking for—a blue vest, in one of the small lockers. It was behind a simple padlock, and the easiest to break open. He quickly produced a padlock shim from his back pocket and had the vest in his hand in seconds—a small redundancy he didn't know he would need, but was certainly glad to have brought alone, just in case.

He slipped it on and pushed past the authorized personnel door. It had been easier than he was expecting.

On the other side of the door, Blake found himself in a long, narrow hallway. Boxes and carts lined the walls in seemingly random spots. Knowing his direction within the building, turning to the right would be the clearest pathway to the offices on the third and fourth floors. He immediately broke right, curing down another corner.

He passed two uniformed officers as he went, and as predicted, neither acknowledged him—the simple sheen of the blue vest being unquestionable to the officers, who probably were used to different employees each month. Even so, Blake know it was only a matter of time before the cafeteria lady returned.

The hallway led him towards a flight of stairs, and he rushed towards the third floor. However, as he pulled on the doorknob towards the office cubicles, the door wouldn't budge. Next to the door, a simple card swipe was required for admittance.

"Can I help you?" A voice came from behind Blake, startling him. He turned around to find another uniformed officer.

"I'm so sorry," Blake started. "We ran out of coffee beans downstairs. You wouldn't happen to have any in the break room, would you?"

The officer was clearly questioning the story, but after a moment, moved to swipe his card. The door beeped open.

"We might," he said, moving past Blake and into the office space. Blake quickly followed.

He found himself in a long hallway, and surrounded by cubicle on either side. This was the side of the military he had chosen to steer clear off—as well as the side the greater public wasn't too aware of. Most people seemed to have the inclination that service involved bombs and killing terrorists, when it mostly consisted of running paperwork, calling different departments, and killing time. After his time in the field ended, Blake turned down the same opportunity Dustin and his other squad mates had been afforded. After he had meet Casey, the idea of sticking around seemed so counterintuitive.

And yet, here he was, back again.

The officer led Blake past these cubicles and into a side room. A fridge, a counter, and a sink lined one side of the room, while the other held a table, with a considerable amount of coffee grinds.

"I don't know what you guys serve downstairs," the officer joked, "but it's usually better than this shit."

"Thank you," Blake said. Luckily enough, the officer left without another word, and Blake found himself alone in the break room.

He tossed the blue vest into the office trash can, then grabbed a few paper plates and tossed them in as well, covering it. He straightened his tie, fixed himself a coffee, and left the break room.

His earlier thought to come into the V.A. office with a close shave and a clean business attire had not been for naught—with the coffee in his hand, he looked no different than several of the other workers. The only thing left to do was find Dustin's office.

Blake passed cubicle after cubicle—different men and women of the armed forces, all now working tirelessly on computers, not bothering to look up at him. After a while, the cubicles ended near the back of the building, leading to actual offices.

These offices seemed to be reserved for the most prestigious of men around the state. Blake recognized several of the names etched onto the doors—from different men he had served with to several he had served under. Each office had its own door, as well as a small window to look in and out of.

Finally, Blake found it; a door near the end of the hallway left wide open, with the name *Dustin Barnes* etched into it. He did a double take, and entered the room.

Dustin seemed to keep his office clean and tidy. The desk was covered in minimal decorations and knick knacks, including a photo Blake recognized. He sat himself in the office chair and picked it up.

Behind the frame glass was a photo of Blake, Dustin, and the rest of his squad out in Afghanistan. Blake couldn't help but smile as he looked to the tents that made up his home for so many months. He and Dustin had spent many days shooting the shit with Jordan and the other men, waiting for the next mission, the next assignment. They used to joke that it was hell on earth, but Blake had never regretted going. Not even for a second.

Because towards the left of the photograph, standing next to Blake, a beautiful woman stood and smiled brighter than the rest of them, happy to be standing in her army medical uniform. She had saved him from that hell on earth, and she was the reason Blake had gone this far.

Blake set the photo down and turned next to the computer. Perhaps just after his retirement, the complexity and counterintuitive nature of the military network would have confused him, but he had learned much about computers since then. He quickly opened up the registry of buildings in current used without so much as a single misstep. Dustin had been kind enough to leave the computer signed in, and had made it that much simpler.

On the registry were the names Blake had expected to see. Various forts and reservations he had paid visits to over the years: *Drum, Hamilton, West Point.* Nothing new from what it seemed. Maybe if there was some way to ensure he was really looking at the complete list?

Blake dug deep into Dustin's files, scanning through the endless repeat documents and disorganization, but it felt fruitless. Any of the network files would certainly not contain information so sensitive it would require conspiracy to cover it, but maybe Roger had a point from earlier—what if there was some sort of higher access chain?

The only way Blake could access such a thing was via email—luckily, Dustin's client was already open. He quickly searched the bulk of the thousands of emails with any terms he could think of; complex, base, operations...none of it were returning searches.

Blake thought to himself for a moment before trying something strange; he opened the search bar, and entered "relocation" into the computer.

More than a few emails were returned.

Blake dug through four or five before anything interesting came up—one from an email that was more letters than numbers. With the subject line empty, the email was short:

Ensure relocation by the 25th. Otherwise, an immediate summons will be issued to Ithaca location.

Ithaca?

"Why shouldn't I call security?" Dustin's voice came from behind Blake. Blake's head lowered slightly and let out a breath. Dustin continued: "I should've known this was what you were planning."

Blake turned around to see a very angry Dustin, standing in the doorframe with takeout in his hand. The lights were still off in his office, and it was hard to see his former friend, who looked to the computer screen. "Dustin—"

"We talked about this. I told you to *let it go.*"

"You think I'm going to give up on my wife because you think I'm going too far with it?" Blake asked. "Jesus Christ, Dustin. Who the hell do you think I am?"

"What you're doing is breaking the law," Dustin said. "Ethical violations, moral violations, any and all retirement benefits you'd ever get would be gone. All for what? Looking for a building?"

"You think I care about the money? About the fact that what I'm doing is illegal?"

"Clearly, you don't," Dustin said. "You have ten seconds to leave before I call security."

Blake stood up from the chair. "We've been through too much shit for you to think I can't tell you're hiding something. And having retired men try to convince me to move to Florida isn't going to change that. If I ever find out you're preventing me from finding my wife, you've got more than your fucking desk job to worry about."

Blake moved past Dustin and moved towards the exit of the building. He didn't look back. In fact, he was almost at the door into the staircase when he felt a hand grab him on the shoulder.

"Blake, wait," Dustin said. He seemed to wait until Blake re-positioned himself towards him before speaking. "There's a lot you don't know about, and there's a very good reason for you to stop now."

"What are you talking about?" Blake nearly growled.

"I can't prevent you from searching for the truth," Dustin said, "but I can't help you either. Believe me, if I knew where she was, I'd tell you."

Blake couldn't believe what he was hearing. He pointed to the computer. "Ithaca?" he asked.

"Maybe, I don't know," Dustin said in a whisper. "I've never been. From what I hear, you never want to go." He looked around; no one was in sight. "I know two things— one, there's a complex near Ithaca. I've heard some of the higher-ups talking about it. People who go usually don't come back around. I don't know what's there, but it's the only building I know that's off any official books."

"And the second thing?"

Dustin's face narrowed. "That people know you're looking for her."

***

Several hours later, Blake slammed his fist repeatedly into Roger's front door. It took a whole fifteen seconds before the door swung open.

"What the hell is your problem?" A shirtless and clearly tired Roger said, standing in the doorframe.

Blake's voice was cool and focused. "Pack your bags. We leave at six tomorrow morning. Be ready to be gone for a few days."

"Wh-what?" Roger asked. "Going where?"

But Blake had already turned, and was heading back downstairs. He had a long, sleepless night ahead of him to plan.

"Ithaca."

7

Ithaca was several hours north and west of New York—far beyond the sprawling cityscapes that made up Blake's everyday life, and deep into the rural hills of what made up the most of the state. Manhattan Island was just a small part of what made up the 'real' New York, and as the cities turned to suburbs turned to fields outside of Blake's car window, he felt a strange sort of kinetic energy.

This was the first time traveling far out of the urban sprawl since Casey left.

"Shit," Roger muttered next to Blake, in the passenger seat. He had dozed off almost immediately after they had left the city, and brushed aside the wrappers and crumbs that lay on his lap onto the floor. He stretched out his arms. "Where are we?"

"Whitney Point," Blake said, looking out at the signs. This far into the countryside, it was small town after small town—each different, but in many ways, exactly the same. "I think we're about an hour out, maybe less."

Roger brushed himself off and sat up in the seat, readjusting. "So, what are looking for, here? Maximum security facilities? Armored trucks?"

"This isn't a movie, Roger," Blake shot off. "That's not how the armed forces work."

"Well then, how does it work?"

Blake sighed. "Look, in order to transport that many people, you need the infrastructure to shuttle bodies in and out of the complex. Truck access roads, shuttle bays, sufficient security measures, etcetera. Whatever is reasonable, then doubled for redundancy's sake."

Roger was silent for a long moment, then responded. "You don't believe it."

"What?"

"Anything you're saying," Roger continued. "You don't think we're going to find anything out here. I can hear it in your voice."

"You don't even know who I am," Blake said. He locked his eyes onto the road. "And why the hell would I be driving you up here if I didn't think we'd find anything?"

"Because there's a chance?"

Blake softened. Roger, for all his lethargy and delusions, wasn't wrong. "I'm a man of reason," Blake understated. "And reasonably, no, this doesn't make any sense."

"So why come out here?" Roger asked.

"Because, reasonably, if there's any chance I could figure out what happened to my wife—if there's just a shadow of a doubt on whether or not she died that night, or got sold off to God knows where...I have to find out."

The car was silent for several minutes afterward.

"It made my family crazy, not knowing what happened to Sam."

Blake turned to Roger. "Who?"

"My sister," Roger said. He seemed to relax more as he talked. "Sam. She actually went missing in Central Park back in the seventies. Afterwards, Mom and Dad couldn't forgive themselves. We spent years trying to figure out answers to questions we just didn't know to ask. Me and

Mom would go to Central Park every weekend for a decade. She would always say it was just to see the flowers, but I still think she was looking for Sam."

Roger bent down and picked up a bottle of soda he had left lying on the floor, and took a large swig. "Anyways, Dad passed of pancreatic cancer in the nineties, and a few years later, Mom passed, too. The doctors couldn't figure out what took her...I guess it was just a broken heart. My uncle was my only family in the area for a long time, before I came over to find him hanging from a rope."

"Christ," Blake muttered. "You know, we don't have to talk about ourselves if—"

"No, it's fine," Roger interrupted. "My point is, this kind of guilt that you're weighing on yourself...it'll kill you, if you let it."

Blake thought for a moment.

"Let's just find this place."

***

They arrived in downtown Ithaca by lunchtime—if you could even call it 'downtown.' A small grid of buildings and small restaurants were all that surrounded a sea of even smaller homes. It was the sort of quiet living that Casey talked about at night—the sort of town she was from, and the sort of place she wanted to retire to, in the end.

Blake pulled the car over at a small diner and the two of them ate in silence. All the while, Blake observed the people around them, trying to sense a read from anyone he could find.

But it seemed that there was nothing here that was out of the ordinary. People in this town moved with a lack a purpose; a comfort and a lack of incentive. Crime was most likely a third or less of what it was in the city, and for the most part, it seemed that there was nothing in the area that could be theorized as dangerous.

Still, Blake thought about Dustin's words about this place. He knew he would need to circumnavigate the city to be sure if there was much in the area.

"Alright, so we're here," Roger said with a full mouth. "Now what?"

Just as he asked the question, a large truck caught Blake's eye. The unmarked eighteen-wheeler took up a lane and a half of the small country road, and took a sharp left turn, northward bound and out of sight.

"We follow him," Blake said.

"It's just a truck," Roger said. "How do we know it's what we're looking for?

"Government license plate," Blake said. "There isn't a military base for that big a shipment for a hundred miles." He tossed a twenty dollar bill onto the table.

The two climbed into Blake's car and moved quickly to follow the truck. Unfortunately, it was long out of sight by the time Blake could round the same corner, but northward seemed to be the way to go. The road here was worn down in a specific place, more so than the other roads near here. These roads were highly trafficked, and once Blake drove far out of the city, the lanes seemed to widen in order to accommodate trucks.

"He could've just been heading to Syracuse," Roger pointed out another twenty minutes into the drive, seeing the passing road signs. "Pretty sure that's around here."

"No, he would've taken a highway," Blake said. "Not a back route like this. Something feels off about this, and I don't know what it is."

As it turns out, Blake's hunch was right.

About another fifteen minutes north of Ithaca, a large road veered off into the tree line, unmarked and clearly well-used. After making the turn, Blake drove up a large hill, and once he crested it, he could see just what he had been looking for all this time.

Deep in a natural valley, a large brick building stood out in a bald patch of forest. There was nothing but clear and open grass surrounding the complex, and a twelve foot barbed wire fence surrounded it. From this height and distance, Blake was able to see the unmarked truck from earlier, pulling to the far side of the building and moving out of sight. In total, the building was most likely the size of three aircraft carriers—definitely big enough for a human trafficking operation, and certainly big enough to warrant suspicion.

"Holy shit," Roger said, breaking Blake's concentration. "What do you think it is?"

"I don't know," Blake said. He had stopped the car just far enough away and couldn't take his eyes off the complex. It was unlike anything he had ever seen stateside—built like a maximum security prison. "I've never seen covert operations make something like this."

His eyes moved next to where the road led—down towards the building and through two separate security checkpoints. And while there seemed to be nobody about at the moment, Blake shifted the car into gear and began to turn around.

"What, we're just going to leave?" Roger exclaimed. He had turned around in his seat and looked at the complex through the rearview window.

"What did you think we were going to do?" Blake said. "Go to the front door and ask if they have my wife? Your sister?"

"I don't know," Roger said. His voice lowered. "I guess I just never expected to find much out here, either. Certainly not something like that."

"We're going back to Ithaca," Blake said. "We can stay the night at a local hotel, but I don't know what we're going to be able to do about this."

As Blake pulled out onto the main road, an SUV turned towards the complex. Blake kept a close eye on the vehicle as it passed—it was unmarked, with windows tinted black, even on the front windshield. No doubt, it was military as well.

***

That night was spent returning to a local hotel back in Ithaca. After the encounter with the complex just north of town, Blake wasn't really sure what to do next. The idea of breaking into such an establishment was laughable. Something as minimalistic as the Veteran's Affairs office was one thing, but entering this building was going to be impossible. Blake had served enough time to know of the mountains of redundancies and checks in a classified or sensitive area of a hanger or a complex. No, entering that building was going to take nothing short of a miracle.

And it was all beside the fact that Blake hardly believed the building was used for trafficking. The need for a covert operation out here could be explained a thousand different ways in a thousand different scenarios—none of which involved human trafficking.

Roger didn't speak much after their encounter. Perhaps it was because he knew the same fact as Blake, or maybe he just wasn't sure how to approach the situation. Either way, Blake couldn't know for sure. Bringing Roger along had always been a bit of a risk—Blake never typically entered any sort of dangerous situation with a person he didn't fully trust. However, he felt a strange debt to Roger. As much as he didn't want to admit it, Roger's pestering helped Blake make up his mind about sneaking past security in the V.A. Office. And he was also the only other person who had seen the woman in the red dress.

"I'm going for a walk," Blake said, climbing out of the old and firm bed. Roger was next to him, zoned out on the second bed and watching the news. "Be back."

Roger nodded his approval, and soon Blake grabbed his room key and slipped out of the room, onto the outside balcony. He placed his elbows on the railing and looked out from the second story towards the main road.

It was probably around ten at night, and the town was already dead. So strange it was, to go from the city that never sleeps, to this. There was an unholy quiet that consumed the town, and with the knowledge of some sort of facility north of here, he knew exactly why this location had been picked for a covert structure.

But what he couldn't figure out for the life of him, was what exactly they could be doing up here. The fact that Blake's long history with the armed forces meant that the very existence of this place was damning enough, but what else? It didn't mean that these people had taken Casey, or Roger's sister, or dozens if not hundreds of other people. It was lunacy to even consider that possibility.

The uncertainty was going to drive him mad, and he was growing more and more confident that they should just turn back now; head home in the morning and figure out a better way of approaching this. Because right now, it felt more like a dead end than the lead Blake was hoping for.

Far to his left, the faint clicking sound of a woman's heels could be heard pacing towards him. Blake paid it no attention and focused his gaze on the road, until the footsteps grew closer and closer, and then finally, right on top of him.

"You're resilient. I'll give you that much."

Blake turned, and found himself face to face with the woman in the red dress. His thoughts raced almost to a halt, and for a moment, couldn't say a word.

"Mind if I smoke?" The woman asked politely, pulling out a cigarette. Without waiting for an answer, she slipped one into her mouth and flicked on a lighter, sending cigarette fumes into the open air. "They don't sell these back where I'm from, and I know they're bad for you, but damn if they aren't worth the buzz every once in a while." She offered one out to Blake.

"No, I'm fine, thanks," he managed to say.

"Suit yourself," she said. "Helps a bit with the pain, too, although it might just be a placebo. You threw out my neck at Central Park, you know."

Blake couldn't believe what he was seeing, but all sense of shock slowly flowed out of his body. He moved quickly into his colder persona.

"You're going to need to start explaining yourself," he said. The longer she stood there, the more Blake prepared not to let her get away. Not this time.

"Yeah," she said, cold as ice. "I suppose I owe you that much. But not here."

As she started to move away from Blake, he felt himself lock up for a brief second. As if he felt he was on the cusp of some great discovery. The answers he sought may finally come to pass, and they might not be what he was looking for.

The woman in the red dress turned around—her face curious, but alluring. "Well?" She asked. "You coming?"

8

The woman in the red dress led Blake up several flights of stairs, to roof of the hotel. Up here, the rocks that coated the rooftop crunched underfoot as the two moved outward, high above the small town, overlooking the city square.

Blake approached her quickly, not waiting for a moment. "How did you find us?"

"I mean, technically," she started, "you found me. That little visit you paid us this afternoon was obvious enough to alert even the most oblivious of our team. You're lucky I got to you first."

"The complex," Blake said, trailing off.

"You know, for ex-military," she continued, "you sure do know how to leave a damning paper trail. Hundreds of forum posts over the past sixteen months, several visits to the scene of the crime, going so far as to meet with another user in the middle of New York City? Anyone in the know could've easily spotted you. Especially since Roger's been on our radar for decades."

"I'm not interested in how obvious you think my methods are," Blake shot back. "They got me this far, didn't they? So, if you're going to call in the cavalry, I'd suggest you do it."

The woman froze for a second, seemingly not sure how to react. Her face narrowed, and she began to speak in a more formal tone: "You're not quite fully aware of the situation you find yourself in, Mr. Collier. And if you did, I don't think you'd be taking the time to threaten me. You've gotten yourself this far, and I'll give you that much, but perhaps it's time you went back to the city."

"Excuse me?" Blake asked. "You think I've gotten myself this far just to be turned around by some idle threat? You seem to know a lot about me. Are you aware of the things I've done? The crimes I committed in the field of war?"

"You've done a great many things, Mr. Collier," she responded. "Marines tend to do a great many things. I know why Dustin's helping you and why you and Jordan don't talk. I'm not undermining your tenacity."

Blake tried not to react to the news that the woman knew so much about his life. But only a handful of people knew what happened between Dustin, Jordan, and himself. Before he could respond, however, she continued:

"But I *am* giving you a warning, that the rest of this conversation could change your life."

"And I am telling you, that I don't care," Blake said. He refused to show her how disarming she really was. "There isn't much you could tell me that would scare me."

The woman paced towards the edge of the building—close enough to cause Blake to worry that she might jump. However, she instead said took a deep drag of her cigarette, and said into the open air:

"Casey's alive, Blake. Alive and well. I can get you to her, but I don't know if you'll ever be able to come back."

Blake tried to hide his inner emotions, but his head was swimming in possibilities. He mustn't lose control of the situation. Any sort of outburst could prevent him from learning anymore. "And how am I supposed to believe you?"

"Because," she said, "I'm the one that was supposed to keep you from her. Or at least, keep you off of the scent."

Blake wanted to ask a million things more, but luckily, she continued:

"My job—technically—is to keep people like you and Roger away from the possibility of finding where your loved ones had gone. I've been in charge of hundreds of cases—ensured each person who chose to dig deeper than the police reports were met with brick walls and dead ends every step of the way. Just enough to keep them from having to be dealt with…more permanently."

"That complex," Blake asked, approaching her. "What is it?"

"It's a transportation hub, you were right on that end," she said. "But it's not an intermediate that people move in and out of. People go in, sure, but they don't come out. Not here."

"And where do they go?"

"Somewhere you might deem incomprehensible," she said. She turned around and looked Blake directly in the eyes. "Somewhere you've never even heard of or ever considered in the realm of possibility. A place willing to play exorbitant amounts of money to replace the ones they've lost."

"You're talking about science fiction," Blake said. "Even if I wanted to, I wouldn't believe it."

"I know," she said. She dropped the cigarette and ground it into the rocks. "That's why I'm going to have to show you, instead. That is, if you're willing to go."

"To the military complex?"

"Farther than that," she said. "But you and your friend need to know that there's a good chance that it's a one-way trip. Nobody like yourself has ever crossed over. When they find out about it—and they will—it'll mean you'll have an entire world searching for you."

Blake found himself speechless. For all of the reason and rationality in his head, he couldn't come up with a thing to say.

"I'll tell Roger," she said, pacing away from him. "Take a minute to think about it. And, if you want to, you'll find me up here tomorrow night at ten sharp. Don't bring anything you can't take with you in a dead run."

As she walked away, Blake called out to her: "Wait…"

She turned around, smiling. "Tamara."

"Tamara," he repeated. "I think I'll have that cigarette now."

***

Several hours later, sometime deep into the witching hour, Blake and Roger were in the middle of a full-blown argument.

"I don't understand what you're so hesitant about," Blake said. He stood at the other end of the room, near the restroom.

Roger was by the front door, his back to the wall, sitting with his legs sprawled out in front of him. "It's absolutely insane."

"And you're not?" Blake asked. "Look, I get it. It's scary—no, it's fucking *terrifying*. But there's no other way she could've known where we were."

"And what if she's lying?" Roger asked. "What if she's right about us digging too far into this? You know how easy it would be for her to lead us to some back alley and whoever the hell she works for comes out and blows our brains out?"

"Then why the hell lure me to the roof of the hotel just to talk?" Blake asked. "Could've easily killed me up there and raided this room. If they wanted us dead, and if this 'they' really is associated with the military, believe me. We'd be dead."

Roger didn't say much, but Blake couldn't help but continue. "Isn't this what you wanted? A chance to figure out whatever happened to your sister? What tore your family apart? No, the answer isn't coming to us in a goddamned goodie bag, sure, but this is the way forward."

"I'm not you, Blake," Roger said. "I'm a private citizen. All the shit I've ever done has been local, has been indoors, and safe. Coming along would just slow everyone down anyways."

"Honestly, Roger, you're not wrong." Blake said. "It would've been a lot easier for me to just leave you in Manhattan when I found out where this building was. But we got into this together. Your theory was right. You convinced me to look into Dustin and find out how to get this far. You're better with research and patterns than I could ever be. Without you, we wouldn't be here. What's holding you back?"

Roger took in a deep breath. "I don't know." He stood up and faced Blake. "It's so final. If—if Tamara's right, and this is some sort of path into a different world, or whatever…that's it. That's the end of the line. Forget coming back home. Everyone I've ever met would be gone."

"All I know is this," Blake said. "I can only speak for myself, and if there's just a modicum of a chance for me to see my wife again, I couldn't really give a damn whether or not I come back. And you're going to have to ask yourself the same question about your sister."

Roger hesitated to speak again—instead making his way to the blinds and looking outside. Blake wasn't sure if it was fear that kept him some simply agreeing, or that the idea of finding his sister had eventually just become more comfortable unresolved.

"I want to find her first," Roger said—a finality in his voice. This was non-negotiable. "I want to know you're not going to use me and that's the only way I can know for sure."

Blake wanted to be mad at Roger. To try and find someone Roger hadn't seen since he was a child? Somebody missing for decades versus finding Casey? It was ridiculous to even assume it would be similar.

But, Blake really couldn't blame him. Being in Roger's position, there was no way of knowing what Blake's true intentions were. Maybe Roger thought Blake was simply going to need him as leverage, or as bait. This way, they could both find some sort of viable way to gain each other's trust.

"Alright, Roger," Blake sighed. "We'll find her first."

***

The daylight came and went quickly, as Blake and Roger spent what could likely be their last day in Ithaca shopping for basic supplies, and discussing some of the tactics Roger may need to learn if he was to enter a dangerous situation as they attempted to find their loved ones. To attempt to train Roger to a status where he could be complimentary to Blake was laughable—Blake's main goal was to make sure Roger didn't get himself killed.

After several hours, however, Roger excused himself for a long walk, and Blake had the room to himself. He quadruple checked everything in each of their bags—both tailor made to their own needs and ability to carry the weight. Obviously, as a well-trained man, Blake had a pack nearly double the size of Roger's.

Inside were dry rations, MRE's, and other survival kits they could find in the local military surplus store. On top of that, blankets, clothes, and other personal effects filled up the rest of the bags. Blake had spent the remainder of the cash he had for this trip on comfortable, versatile clothing he wouldn't mind having to spend a few days in.

The more he thought about what Tamara said about exactly *where* they were going, the less he understood. It was a gut feeling and a blind trust that instilled in him enough initiative to travel with her.

Roger arrived back at the room a few minutes before ten, and both of them loaded up, locked the door behind them, and arrived onto the rooftop.

As promised, Tamara stood—poised and alone, dressed in an active service military uniform. Although, the ranks and insignias were somehow foreign to him...

"Looks like you're both prepared," Tamara said, her eyes looking to their backpacks and gear. "Last chance to turn back."

Blake did not hesitate. "Let's go."

Tamara let out a small smile. "Leave your phones here," she said. "From this point on, anything that's trackable needs to be discarded or destroyed."

The men complied, and from the rooftop, Tamara led the two men back down the stairs to the parking lot, where an unmarked SUV was left dormant. She opened the back trunk to reveal a large metal enclosure, hidden from sight from anyone outside of the car.

"This is one of the vehicles they use for human transport," Tamara explained, opening the outer wall. "It's made out of the same material as lead aprons for x-rays. It keeps anything short of a physical search of the car from discovering anything or anyone inside."

Blake shook the thought of Casey being forced to ride in one of these. "And you don't think they'll be checking this physically as soon as we arrive at the complex?" He asked.

"The complex runs on an automated system," she said. "They only do searches if there are people inside here needing to be verified. You're going to have to trust me on this one, Collier."

Blake pushed away the questions he might have raised and begrudgingly climbed inside of the enclosure.

After Roger had done the same, the space became small and cramped—Blake had barely enough room to hold his legs close to his chest.

"When I close this box, there's going to be no ventilated air and complete darkness. Control your breathing and movements. This can easily become a hotbox."

And with that, Tamara lifted the enclosure's fourth wall, trapping the two of them into complete darkness. Blake could hear her latch the locks, close the doors, and move to sit in the driver's seat of the car. The floor on which they sat vibrated softly as Blake could feel the car begin its drive. "Point of no return," Blake heard Roger mutter.

Twenty long minutes later, or at least by his assessment, Blake could feel the car come to a complete stop. Outside the car, a long, drawn-out rattle felt as if it had shaken the car itself.

The first checkpoint.

The car rolled forward. Next would be the secondary checkpoint, and typically the more exhaustive one. For the first time in quite some time, Blake felt a tinge of true fear run through him. The sort of fear you only ever feel in a foxhole, and one that Blake last felt the last time he was on the wrong side of a barrel.

The car slammed to a stop outside, sending Blake's head smashing into the forward wall of their cell. He could feel the heat from Rogers shallow breaths, warming the both of them and further stretching out the amount of time they seemed to be spending in this prison.

A few voices seemed to shout from outside the car, and then all was quiet again. The problem was, they weren't moving. Complete silence took over the inside of the compartment, and Blake started to think of a few exit strategies. What if they opened the compartment and Blake was able to escape? Would he want to? Would they take him to where they had taken Casey years before?

Blake was lucky enough to have to continue the thought, as the car rolled forward, and within another minute or so, parked. He could hear Tamara's footsteps pace to the back of the car, open the trunk, and finally, open their compartment, sending Blake's entire vision into a white haze and cool air rushing inside.

While his vision slowly cleared, he could make out Tamara, and a clear parking lot behind her. Even further back was the wire fencing Blake had noticed when he had scoured this place.

They were inside.

9

"*God*," Roger muttered. Blake couldn't see him very well, but could make out Tamara's blurred form shushing him.

"Shut up and listen to me," Tamara said in a low tone. "There isn't much time. Shift change happens every night at 23:00. Once that time hits, our window to move inside is only twelve minutes."

Blake climbed out of the car, shaking off the pins and needles from being cramped for so long. "What time is it now?"

"22:53."

Now outside and with his full vision out, Blake scanned his surroundings.

It seemed as though Tamara parked on the far side of the complex, with most of the lights out in this section. They were also in a small enclosed section of the building, with a large awning covering them.

"What's this?" Roger said, looking up at the awning.

"It's the same color as the roof," Tamara said. "You can fit twelve trucks under here easily and still be hidden from any of the satellite feeds. From the internet, this place just looks like another building."

Blake was both impressed and horrified at the scale of this place. Now that he was this close, he could see how easily the building could house hundreds, even thousands of people.

"Through these doors," Tamara said, casting a finger to the steel plated door to her left. "Are the main offices. There's two distinct sections of this building. Everything above ground would easily pass an inspection, and regularly does by anyone not in the know. Everything *below* ground, however, is a different story. It currently only handles a fraction of the bodies than it can, but other forces are preparing for mass transit by the thousands."

"There's a basement?" Roger asked.

"More than that," Tamara continued, "underneath us is a huge labyrinth. Whenever people arrive here, they're usually processed for a few days. Heavily sedated, and highly guarded. But once they're ready, they move to the heart of the building—the Terminus. That's the bridge."

"I don't understand," Blake said. "Why sedate them? And what's the bridge?"

"I wish I could explain all of this to you," Tamara said, "but I don't have the time. It's best if you see it to understand."

Just as she said so, a small beeping noise emanated from her pocket. She pulled out her phone and pressed a few buttons.

"Alright," she said. "Let's move."

Tamara led the way forward, opening the steel door and beckoning Blake and Roger to come inside.

The door led them to a surprisingly mundane hallway. Bright fluorescents painted the walls a strange blue tint, while endless doors lined either side of the wall towards more and more hallways.

Silently, the three moved past several of these doors, giving Blake the opportunity to scan the walls for names he may recognize. Unfortunately, not a single door seemed to be marked, and each seemed to require biometric authentication to open.

Tamara took a sharp turn to the left, leading herself and the others towards a red door—a clear standout from the others. She scanned three fingers and entered a long passcode, and the door buzzed open.

Once Roger closed the door behind them, Tamara turned around to face the two men.

"Once we head down this staircase," she said, "even the smallest sounds could attract attention. And once our cover is blown, we're not getting out of here. No trials, no lawyers."

"Keep it down," Blake said, annoyed. "Got it. Let's keep moving."

Tamara nodded and kept them moving.

Next, the group moved down several flights of stairs, down to what Blake estimated to be at least two hundred feet underground. Finally, after the last flight of stairs, the group poured out into an area unlike anything Blake had ever seen.

Instead of the traditional hallways, down here, the walls and ceilings gave way, and the group found themselves in what appeared to be a massive underground cave, with catwalks connecting the various parts of the structure. Blake could see several hundred feet both above and below him, with varied isolated rooms, infrastructure to house thousands, and not a single person in sight.

At least, not yet.

The group walked with a very light foot—as each footfall rang out into the open air of the cave. They traveled slowly down even more stairs, and eventually approached what Blake assumed to be the central location—a large floating, building-like structure in the center of it all. It seemed to be the size of a small house, made entirely of plated steel, and had various catwalks all heading to several entrances.

Another door and another biometric authentication later, Tamara led the two men inside.

"We should be relatively safe in here," she said, using her normal voice. "But I'm going to need a moment to activate the Terminus."

"What are you talking about—" Blake tried to ask, but his eyes had turned to the center of the room, and what he saw left him speechless.

The entire building was hollow, and wiring and generators lined every wall. Huge sources of power all led towards the same, small circular ring in the center of the room. It seemed about six feet tall, a foot or so thick, and hellishly dangerous.

"It's a gateway," Roger exclaimed. He approached without hesitation, his neck craning up and down the mess of wiring. "It's a portal to another world!" His eyes shined—he had been right, the whole time. Something very sister had taken his sister and Casey.

"That's a pretty simplistic way of putting it," Tamara said, moving towards what looked to be a control console. "But yes…it is."

"I can't believe what I'm seeing…" Blake said, trailing off. "How much power does this thing need?"

"More than the entire city of Ithaca," she answered. "It's a wonder why no one's figured out the power plant out here is three times the size it needs to be."

She had been right, yesterday on the rooftop. Blake hadn't believed her. He wasn't sure what to believe, in fact, after he had heard what she had told him, but now that it was looking at his straight in the face, it only meant one thing to him.

Casey was alive, and somewhere on the other side of that device, he would find her.

"How long does it take to get online?" he asked.

"It's activated both from here and a sister control panel on the other side of the Terminus," she said. "Either side can turn it on, but if one side turns it on without the other, it takes double the amount of time to boot up."

"Meaning?" Roger asked.

"Meaning, at least a few minutes."

As Tamara finished speaking, a strange rattling sound shot out overhead. Within moments, the emergency lights above them were activated, painting the entire inner room a deep crimson red. Sirens began to wail.

They had been found out.

Without so much as a second thought, Blake bolted from his current position towards the door. Opening it and looking out, he could see the very same catwalks they had traversed down in order to arrive here, now occupied by several armed guards. He closed the door and locked it before giving them a chance to spot him.

"We've got about thirty seconds before those guards arrive," Blake shouted out to the other two. His eyes moved next to a large cabinet against the wall, near the door. "Roger, help me with this!"

Roger broke from his frozen position and sprinted over to Blake, grabbing at the opposite end of the cabinet as Blake began to push. The cabinet was heavy—probably filled to the brim with wires and paperwork. Blake stopped it in front of the door, but knew it would only buy them another few seconds at most.

"Can you access the power grid from there?" Roger called out to Tamara. "If you can shut off the overhead lights outside, it could slow them down!"

"There's no time," Tamara said. For the first time since they had meet her, she seemed nervous; scared, even. Her hands flew over the console and seemed to move with an otherworldly force. "Get in front of the Terminus, now! I can speed up the reaction time, but it's going to be unstable. It'll only be a few seconds before it shuts off again."

A loud bang reverberated from the door, shuttering the cabinet and threatening to knock it over. Blake looked to the Terminus, which seemed to be sparking and surging to life. "We'll make it work!"

Blake and Roger ran towards the Terminus, abandoning their post at the door. This close to the machine, the sounds of the sirens were deafening.

"Remember!" Tamara called out. "Once you're on the other side, you're not out of the woods yet!"

"You're not coming?" Roger asked. As he did so, a massive swell of wind radiated from the center of the Terminus—a gust stronger than the average wind turbine. Both he and Blake were forced to dig their heels into the ground, and try to hear Tamara over the torrent of noise.

"No time!" She shouted. Tamara raised a hand in the air and slammed it onto the console. "Somebody has to man the controls!"

A brilliant flash of light shot out from the center of the Terminus, momentarily blinding Blake in a white light. The empty space inside the arc of the terminus was now filled with a swirling, purplish-red haze. It looked as if he was about to enter a miniature galaxy.

Behind them, with a loud crack, the door finally gave way, and several security guards began to pour in.

"Go!" Tamara shouted. "Find *HALO!*"

Blake turned and took several uneasy steps forward, into the vortex.

"Find HALO!"

The steps became easier and easier, until finally Blake's body lurched forward, as if gravity had suddenly switched directions. The noise grew to a cacophonous roar, and Blake could see nothing but whiteness.

And then all at once, the sounds stopped, the forces gave way, and Blake could see nothing at all.

10

Blake felt himself toss and turn several times in the dark, before being thrown onto the ground again. His eyes opened to see what looked to be the Terminus. Within it, a body seemed to assemble from nothing, and was also flung forward, onto Blake.

Roger and Blake both found themselves on the other end of the Terminus—wherever that may be.

Blake pulled himself from Roger, who seemed to writhe in pain of being thrown around so violently. Blake himself wasn't feeling much better; aching with a strange sort of feeling unlike he had ever experienced before. A feeling as if he had been pulled apart and placed back together again.

Shaking off the feeling, Blake scanned the room he stood within. Instead of the cold, industrial walls of the complex, the walls were glass, and the floor made of cheap carpet. Large windows stood behind the Terminus, and Blake rushed to look outside of them.

As he stepped forward to look, the bright rays of a morning sun shone into his eyes, he blinked rapidly, attempting to get used to the new source of light. What appeared as his vision cleared was nothing short of indescribable.

Somehow, they had found themselves hundreds of stories in the air, in what appeared to be one of many skyscrapers in a city. The other buildings that stood nearby soared over this floor, even higher, stretching into the clouds. These buildings had visual screens on them—projections of products, tools and appliances unlike anything he had ever seen.

The cityscape seemed to stretch for miles and miles, far beyond the horizon that he could see. Even bigger than New York, even larger, and even more technologically advanced.

Blake found himself in another world.

"Where the hell are we?" Roger asked, approaching the window. As Roger took it all in, Blake tried to shake off the revelation and look more so to the interior of the room he found himself in.

The floor he was on seemed to hold, aside from the Terminus, various desks and computers—although he found himself unable to recall which sort of devices he was looking at. The building on this floor, with each wall being completely made up of glass, could be seen throughout, and Blake quickly charted a path towards the only possible escape route—the opaque shaft running down the center of the building, no doubt where the elevators would be.

"We need to keep moving," Blake said, turning to Roger. "We don't know who knows about our arrival."

"Yeah, yeah," Roger muttered quickly. As Roger reproached Blake, he seemed to wipe at his face, blinking heavily. Perhaps the shock of being right, after all this time, was enough to move him. Something he had always known, but finally been vindicated.

And if Blake thought about it hard enough, it would've been enough to shock him to the core, but now, there was no time. They needed to escape if Blake ever wanted the chance to find Casey.

The two men weaved their way past the seemingly-empty offices, and approached what Blake thought to be the elevator shaft. However, there was just one problem:

Not a single button could be found.

"Blake?" he heard Roger say next to him.

"I don't know," Blake shot back. "Just start looking."

Escape was the only thing on Blake's mind at the moment. Regardless of the shock of the arrival, it was all for nothing if they couldn't even make it out of the building. He stepped forward, running his fingers against the polished metal, searching for some sort of device or switch.

Suddenly, a neon dot emanated from the wall, about eight feet up. The two of them both took a step back, and watched as the dot stretched in either direction, then descended towards the floor. It appeared to be outlining an elevator door. As it turned out, the elevator doors were so flush with the wall, it was as if there were no doors to be found. Soon, it would open, and Blake had no idea what would be found inside.

"Come on," Blake said, grabbing Roger and pulling him aside. The two of them slipped around the corner, waiting to see what came next.

From his limited vantage point, Blake could see the wall open, and a few men stepping out from where no door had been before. There were five of them—each dressed in sharp, black clothing, and moved directly towards the Terminus, some fifty feet away. Blake waited until they had reached a considerable distance before pulling Roger with him towards the elevator door.

The two stepped inside what appeared to be a standard elevator—minus the strange, revealing opening. On a touchscreen monitor to the right of the door, Blake could see a model of the entire building from afar. He pressed the ground floor, and the doors quickly shut. So far, so good.

Perhaps this new environment wouldn't be so difficult to maneuver.

"Tamara said something before we walked into that…thing," Roger said. "We need to find something. Something called *HALO*."

"We don't have time to start looking for anything other than an escape route," Blake said. "We don't know where the hell we are. As soon as we're out of this building, we can arrange some sort of plan." As he finished speaking, the doors opened to the ground floor, and the two stepped out without another word.

This room most closely resembled a lobby in many of the hotels back in Brooklyn. Clean, modern walls and wide-open spaces. Blake glanced behind him to see the elevator doors closing, and the light outline of the door fade away, obscuring the elevators once more into the walls.

Several people paced around the large space in front of them—many mostly adorned in thick suits and black ties. Everything around them was off-kilter; almost as if they were walking inside an artist's representation of what their world actually was.

"Excuse me," came a voice from behind Blake, causing him to turn around. Before him was a beast of a man, who was trailed by several others. "What department are you from again?"

"Oh, we were just getting directions," Blake diverted, looking to Roger, who had already frozen in place. In their backpacks and pseudo-stealth outfits, they were already sore thumbs in the area. And Blake had a feeling this conversation wasn't going to end well. "We took a wrong turn a few blocks back."

The man was not buying it: "You mind if we see your ID?"

The men behind the larger man were already attempting to form a perimeter around them. It was now or never.

Blake swung a sharp uppercut directly into the man's face, sending him straight to the floor. Luckily enough, the quick action was enough to buy just a second, as the other men froze in place.

"*Move,*" Blake said to Roger, and broke into a full-on sprint towards the exit.

He paid no attention to the shouting and commotion behind him, and focused instead on sharp, measured breaths. He pushed the glass door wide open and spilled out into the street.

Almost immediately, he had run straight into several walking citizens, knocking a few to the asphalt. He stood quickly and turned around, just in time to see Roger clearing the door. Only a few feet behind him, the other men were giving pursuit.

Blake took a second to glance up and down the street—here, instead of cars, it seemed that the entire channel between buildings had been occupied by patrons moving in all directions. It was as if Times Square itself had tried to fit itself into Chinatown. On top of that, it was the perfect diversion.

Blake signaled to Roger, and began to push his way past several civilians. Deep into the crowd he moved, not taking a moment to stop and look around. From the center, he could see a set of stairs leading under the ground, and moved right for it.

He descended quickly, hoping for a subway system for an escape. Instead, he nearly found himself run over, as the stairs led straight towards a highway, built underneath the city. Behind him, Roger finally caught up, stopping just short of the interstate.

"Alright," Roger said, breathless. "So, there's no subway."

To his left, Blake could see a parking lot, just off the main road. Several cars remained stopped here.

Blake and Roger both moved in turn towards the cars, ducking behind the nearest one. Blake peered around the corner to see a few of the men entering the underground tunnel, looking around for them.

"What now?" Roger whispered sharply in Blake's ear.

"We need one of them," Blake said.

Behind them, Blake could see around a short, narrow corner, clearly marked with a small, familiar stick figure.

At least the restrooms were the same.

"Get one to follow you to that corner," Blake said. He moved off without waiting to see if Roger would agree, and crawled below the line of cars around the corner. Here was exactly what he had been looking for—a long, narrow hallway, and not a soul in it. The perfect bottleneck.

After about ten long seconds, Roger sprinted around the corner, moving past Blake. Next came one of their pursuers, running right into their trap.

Blake knocked this one out cold before he ever even saw him.

"*The door,*" Blake gestured to Roger, who opened the bathroom door for him. Blake dragged the man's body into the restroom, and locked the door behind them.

"Jesus," Roger said. "Is he going to be alright?"

But Blake wasn't even listening to his partner. He flipped the unconscious man to his back, and reached for a wallet. Within seconds, he produced one, and dug through it.

"Look through this," Blake said to Roger, handing him several bills. He turned his attention next to the cards.

Bits of information helped Blake form an idea of what this world was like. The man had with him a National ID card, several business cards, and a thicker card, marked only with "Reegan Corp," in small letters, in the bottom right corner.

"Well, I *think* it's money," Roger said. Blake turned to him and looked to the bills in his hand—each a different size and color. In whatever currency it was, the two of them had about three hundred dollars. Hopefully, it would be enough.

"We need to keep moving," Blake said. He stood up and kept the wallet with him, and moved for the door.

"We can't just leave him like this," Roger protested.

"Relax. Someone will find him."

Blake pushed past the door and approached the main parking lot with a trained hesitance. Around the corner, the cars sat dormant, and not a single pursuer could be seen. They were clear, for now, but they needed to move far away from here.

11

Once enough time had passed, Blake and Roger were able to slip above ground once more, moving with the flow of the foot traffic far away from the building that they had arrived at. Blake kept a close eye on the buildings nearby, taking a mental note of where they were—especially in the massive, sprawling city.

The entire design of this place was a strange mixture of familiar and foreign. The buildings were stark and cold, but the crowds were cluttered, and people seemed to ebb and flow from each building, overpopulating the streets to their full limit, with no signs of it ever slowing down. As he had discovered earlier, the streets were underground in this world, not above. And for good reason—the foot traffic was pushed to its very limits.

Once they felt they had made enough turns (taking the time to double back several times), Roger pointed out a small hotel off of a small capillary of the main street. They entered inside to find a comfortable, small lobby, empty aside from the concierge.

"How much for myself and my friend, here?" Blake asked the hotel manager.

"Twenty for the night," the man said. "I'll just need some ID on file."

Blake set down fifty. "How about we pay this upfront instead?"

***

The hotel concierge handed both of them keys to a two bed hotel room on the fifth floor. As soon as the door had shut behind them, Roger collapsed onto the bed with a huff.

"What time is it?" He said, muffled by the sheets.

Blake looked outside and compared to his watch—the sky shined as if midday had just begun, but his watch read eight in the morning. They had been awake all night. Blake's eyes turned to the desk between the two beds, which confirmed his intuition and read just past two in the afternoon.

"You ever been jet-lagged before?" Blake asked. When Roger didn't respond, he continued: "You have to stay up until it's nighttime before you can sleep again. If you don't, it's going to be like this for days. We're six hours shifted from our time."

Blake moved forward next and observed the greater surroundings in the area. The hotel room seemed standard enough, even including a view through the fourth wall—a floor to ceiling window that showed most of the city. Along the wall to Blake's left, there was a desk and chair, complete with one of the strange-looking computers he had spotted back in the skyscraper just a few hours ago.

"I'm going back out to the city," Blake said. "Get on the computer and start researching anything you can. Anything we can use to assimilate here."

Roger groaned as he pulled himself from the bed, moving to the computer. "Come back with caffeine."

Blake left the room and moved back to the lobby, before spilling back out into the main city from there.

The streets reminded him of Bagdad, of all places. The constant motion of each individual, everybody knowing exactly where to go with no sense of personal space. Blake could remember what it had been like on his first tour, when he and the others in his squad would have to run reconnaissance in the big city. He, Dustin, and Jordan always took shifts pushing through the piles of bodies, trying to find that one nefarious needle in the haystack of the city. He had always felt that New York had prepared him for so much movement and so many variables, but that first journey to Bagdad had been key in reminding him of the far greater picture beyond his own scope.

This city was as much the same a humbling experience for Blake as an interesting one. Tracking down Sam and Casey was going to be a nightmare if they lived within the city—especially without military-grade access to surveillance and resources. On top of it all, Blake knew better than to think he and Roger were out of the woods yet. The high-grade security on the other side of the Terminus was not for nothing, and while no one seemed to be curious about their intentions now, it was really only a matter of time.

Blake ducked off from the main thoroughfare into what appeared to be a general convenience store. The crowds inside were beginning to have a draining effect on him—the entire day was beginning to be a sensory overload of new sights, sounds, and people. So many things to consider, Blake was beginning to wish he had brought Dustin or some of the other members of his squad to come along.

The convenience store worked like most others, with prices he was happy to produce at the register. He collected a few things he and Roger could eat that night to avoid leaving the apartment, as well as enough caffeine to keep both of them up to plan for the next day's journey. Blake trusted Roger enough to know he'd figure out the next move via the internet, which was a welcome change. In an environment as alien as this, someone steadfast was going to be paramount.

As he checked out his things, a view screen to the right of the register was playing local news. The translucent screen showed the video, as well as the counter behind it, in a disorienting fashion similar to a 3-D movie back home. Blake tried to pay it no mind and focus on the news itself:

"Local officials are still trying to ascertain what exactly happened that night at RDS; a subsidiary of Reegan United. We haven't been able to get a comment from the regional authorities, but rumors are spreading that a guerrilla organization nearby was responsible for the attack, and the deaths of over fifteen employees."

"That's going to be fifteen credits," the cashier said over the video. "Cash or district card?"

"Cash," Blake said, keeping his eyes locked onto the screen and handing the money over. "What's RDS?"

"Not from this province, are you?" the cashier said. He produced the change for Blake and handed him his things. "Reegan Duplicate Services. They've been all over the news recently over these terrorist attacks."

"Thanks," Blake said. He hesitated before leaving, but soon returned to the bustling streets, and made it back to the hotel room.

As he entered, he found Roger effortlessly typing away at the keyboard; his back arched and his face aimed directly at the screen.

"Back up a bit, would you?" Blake said in a dry tone. He set down a canned coffee and started unloading his groceries. "What have you found?"

"Christ, what *haven't* I found?" Roger said back. "This whole city at least is incredibly interconnected. There's information on here you wouldn't believe. Addresses, phone numbers...there's a national registry of individuals for public use. And the computer system is still a GUI, so figuring it out didn't take but a minute."

"How Orwellian," Blake said, noting the surveillance. He sat at the edge of the bed, positioned towards his new partner. "They asked me if I wanted to pay with a state card."

"It's all an integrated system," Roger continued. "Government issued ID, universal currency, automated welfare systems, you name it. This place is highly advanced in terms of how accessible all the information is. This is a goldmine for some of the guys back on that internet forum."

"Any luck with finding Sam or Casey?"

"Not a thing, at least in this district. This whole damn country is a city, just separated out by district. And they don't call it a 'country,' either. The whole world is divided into provinces that operate basically like countries or city-states. And then, each one is sub-divided into districts. And this district is *huge.* It's got to be like at least ten times the size of Staten and Long Island combined."

"That's going to be perfect for us," Blake said. He took mental notes of the governmental systems Roger mentioned. "We'll keep moving for a while to keep out of the line of sight. And that building we ran out of?"

"Owned by Reegan United. They're this big tech conglomerate, but they own pretty much a piece of every market there is. There's a page on them, but everything's really vague. It's all written in this strange corporate speak. Nothing but buzzwords and doublespeak."

"That Terminus was hidden too high up for it to be public knowledge here," Blake continued. He moved to the window, looking out at the buildings and the setting sun. "We're going to have to be careful. If this Reegan corporation is in charge of this, and it's this secret project—"

Blake was cut off by a strange sight out of the window.

Somewhere about three blocks north of the building they currently occupied, a group of armed men moved against the flow of the crowd. None of the other citizens seemed to pay them any mind as they moved from door to door, crawling the city streets.

"I'm reading something that might be helpful here," Roger said behind him. "Something about RDS."

"No time," Blake cut in. "Get your stuff. We're moving out. Now."

Blake collected their things at a breakneck pace as Roger moved towards the window, locking eyes with the looming threat outside.

The two ditched their key cards on the counter, closing the door behind him. They descended the stairs quickly, and moved quickly into the streets.

"You think they're after us?" Roger asked.

"I'm not taking the risk," Blake said. "We need to get as far away from here as we can. Any ideas?"

"There's a low-income district about fifteen miles or so to the south," Roger shouted over the noise of the crowd. "Probably the best bet."

"Lead the way."

Roger moved in front of Blake, leading a swerving path through the city streets. Blake could see behind him in the distance several of the men in black suits continuing to knock on doors. Luckily, with this much foot traffic, getting away was going to be easy.

Staying hidden, however, was going to prove to be *much* harder.

12

Low income, as Roger had described the district south of the center of town, turned out to be a gross understatement.

Blake and Roger arrived late in the evening, and the crowds of the northern district seemed to completely fade to the occasional straggler. The only real noise from here came from the underground roadways, which vibrated the streets on a constant basis.

The tall skyscrapers here seemed to peter out into smaller apartments and liquor stores around every block. In the dark, the streets were painted a neon color from the translucent advertising that hung over and across each building.

This area of town is where Blake could find the first sign of true nature—overgrown grass that stretched from the cracked sidewalks towards the main road, spawning from the darkened alleyways. For all the modern ingenuity of the northern district, down here reminded Blake of the state of the Bronx as a child; a memory that reminded him of the loss of his parents. Such thoughts wouldn't serve him now, so he tried to shake it off as best he could.

He shook off the thoughts and focused on the pathways ahead, thankful that the vehicle traffic lay below them. Because of it, they were able to cover a substantial amount of ground and ensure that nobody was around to watch them do it.

"What a shitty place," Roger muttered, nearly indiscernible from the ambient noise to Blake. The two passed by a strange section of town with words scrawled out in jagged lines on the walls. In spray paint, phrases like 'duplicate scum' and 'unnaturals' were written out amongst the common vulgarity.

"There's got to be some sort of hotel around here," Blake said. "If I could bribe the concierge up north, here should be no problem." He looked over to Roger, who was showing very clear signs of fatigue. Neither of them had a real moment to sleep since Ithaca, which felt like such a long time ago after all that had happened. Blake guessed that they had been awake for well over 30 hours.

After another block or two of wandering, Blake and Roger came across a more vibrant area of the community. Here, the vacant lots gave way to occupied, if not unsavory buildings. Shops and bars lined the streets, and stragglers came up from the underground street system and approached the bars. Lining the main streets, panhandlers held up various signs, begging for credits.

One such building was a green and red corner bar, busy and vibrant with customers and other night-dwellers. Blake approached with Roger close behind, and the two entered to the loud noise of strange, electronic music. "We'll ask about a room in here," Blake said to Roger, and approached the bar.

Several other patrons to the bar shuffled to the side to make room for Blake—an unexpected kindness. The bartender took notice of the new customer, and finished serving a few of the others before approaching.

"If you wanna open a tab, I need district ID," the man said in a gruff accent Blake couldn't recognize. "Otherwise, what is it?"

"I'm new here," Blake admitted. "I'm looking for a place to stay. Somewhere off-grid?"

"Nowhere's off-grid," the bartender replied. "Although they don't ask too many questions a few blocks south of here. There's a couple of spots there that'll put you up."

"Thanks," Blake said. "Oh, and one more thing. You know anything about a HALO?"

The bartender immediately began to walk away. "Never heard of it." He kept himself busy enough to drive Blake back away from the bar.

"So?" Roger asked. He had stood a few feet back.

"We're going farther south," Blake explained. "There's a few places there we can keep quiet at."

Blake and Roger stepped out of the bar without further incident, and kept moving past some of the other ruffians that lined this area. The overpopulation of this sprawling city was showing once more, and Blake and Roger struggled to keep moving past the cries of homeless and desperate.

"Right over here," one such panhandler said, pulling Roger's arm towards a particularly darkened building. "Good times, no surveillance, promise! Just five credits!"

"I'm good," Roger forcefully said to the man, pulling his arm back. He turned next to Blake. "Let's get the hell out of here."

The two walked for some time in the dark before either spoke again. "You think Dustin knew about this place?"

"I doubt it," Blake admitted. "And if he did, he certainly wouldn't have ever come. This place freaks me out more than any slums we ever waded through."

"And which slums were that?"

Blake grimaced at the thoughts in his mind about his time in the field. Sure, he was good at it—better than most. But the good times he had over there were outweighed by the horrors he had seen. "I've been to a lot of places, Roger," Blake said. "Aleppo, Damascus…places that aren't safe. Places more complicated than people give them credit for."

"So why does this place scare you more?"

"Because I knew what I was getting into," Blake said. "And I don't know what the hell is out here."

And it was true. Blake had been briefed every time he moved out into the field. He had Dustin and Jordan and the other men at his side at all times. Here, the unknown was what scared him the most. There was briefing to be had.

Blake was about to speak again when a blinking light struck at his eyes. Lifting them to the sky, he could see a spotlight overhead, coming directly from a helicopter high above the streets.

All around them, the streets cleared out. People scattered like roaches across the pavement, heading for any door that hadn't already been closed and locked. Without enough information and in fear of being caught, Blake followed their lead, and took off with Roger down the street.

"*Attention! Please remain where you are!*" A loud, automated voice blared from the helicopter. "*This is a routine checkpoint. Please provide district identification. Attention! Please remain where you are!*"

Blake and Roger followed the crowds of people as best they could, but the streets cleared out before they could find considerable shelter. The two found themselves to be some of the last left on the streets by the time the helicopter was beginning to land.

"Back here!" Roger shouted. Blake turned his head to see Roger, just as he ducked into a back alleyway. He moved into it without hesitation, scanning the nearby buildings for any surveillance. As with the northern district, there seemed to be cameras everywhere, even back here. Halfway down the darkened alley, the overhead lights seemed to cut on, revealing their location. It was as if the city itself was alive and searching for them.

Luck was not on their side, and the two came out into a dead end behind several businesses—the only shelter seeming to be several dumpsters. Blake ran to try the back doors, but each were locked fast.

Looking up, Blake could see windows stretching for many stories above them. The windows on the second floor were barred shut, but the third floor windows were open and free.

"Help me with this!" Blake shouted to Roger. He moved to the nearest of the dumpsters and began pushing it closer to the wall, towards the windows.

Following his lead, Roger pushed his entire weight into it and together, the relatively empty dumpster moved with a groan, striking the wall.

Blake climbed on top of the dumpster, which reached just three feet below the second story windows. He grasped at the bars and pulled himself up them, now several feet from the top of the dumpster.

He reached for the window, but to his surprise, the glass was flush with the wall and lacked a ledge—a strange peculiarity of this world, much like the flatness of the elevators. He could only just barely brush his fingers against the glass, and there was no way to get a grip here. There was no way he could break it like this.

He jumped down to the roof of the dumpster, where Roger had just climbed up. "Your backpack," he said. "Pull out the rope I gave you." As Roger did so, Blake produced a carabiner from his backpack and tied it to the rope. Two things he was glad he purchased back in Ithaca.

He stood on top of the dumpster and swung the carabiner high above his head, using the rope as leverage. Within two tries, the carabiner struck the window at high speed, shattering it easily.

Blake jumped back up onto the barred windows of the second story and pushed himself high enough to get a grip on the inside of the building. He grimaced as he felt shards of glass cut deep into his hands, but was able to maneuver himself through the window. He turned back towards the window as soon as he entered it, giving Roger a helping hand up.

Both found themselves inside a darkened office space. Familiar cubicles lined the walls of this particular open concept room, and enough streetlight shone through the windows to give them a clear path to see.

Blake tore a strip from his shirt, wrapping it over his bleeding hand. He winced as the fabric dug deep into his bleeding flesh, but there was no time to take proper care of it now. Without bothering to look behind them, both Blake and Roger kept moving.

About fifty feet ahead of them, a clearly labeled stairway seemed like the best course of action. They full-on sprinted towards it, making sure to keep far enough away from the window to prevent any stray bullets from striking them.

As Blake closed the gap and opened the door, he took the opportunity to turn around. From his perspective, just behind Roger, a second window shattered—this one by a bullet. It was only another couple of seconds before a man in full riot gear was climbing inside.

Roger finally made it to the stairway and moved ahead of Blake. Blake followed close behind, moving down the stairs as fast as he could. The pounding of footsteps above them signaled that whoever was after them had several men where they had been standing just moments ago.

They moved past the second and first floors, and found that the stairway continued downwards, towards what was presumably the underground freeway. As they continued, gunshots fired down the gaps in the stairs, striking the metal guardrails and ricocheting bullets throughout the stairwell. The men had arrived and were shooting downwards, in hopes of striking them.

Blake and Roger burst through the bottom door, glad to be out of the line of fire, and soon came across a parking lot as expected—right alongside the still-busy underground freeway.

What they were not expecting was an unmarked black vehicle, with several masked men and women in front of it.

"Wait, Blake!" one of the masked men called out, before Blake could think what to do next. "Blake! Roger!"

The both of them were stunned to silence.

"We're not them," the man said, his voice muffled by the mask.

"How do you know our names?" Roger asked.

"I can explain, but not here," the man continued. He pointed to the truck, where several of his fellow soldiers were already climbing in. "You need to come with us, or those men will kill you on sight."

Blake turned to Roger, and for a moment, time seemed to stop.

He found himself in one of the many split-second decisions that had come to define his career as a Marine. Moments where the decision to move in one direction or the other was just as important as the decision whether or not to pull the trigger. The decision to go with these men now could mean the difference between seeing their loved ones again, and dying just moments from now.

All things considered, Blake chose the former.

He moved forward, ducking his head as he climbed into the back of the vehicle. Roger came behind him, and two of the other masked people closed the doors behind them. The truck immediately lurched forward, accelerating fast. It turned into the underground merge lane and sped up far faster than either Blake or Roger had ever experienced. The truck seemed to move well over a hundred miles per hour as it merged into the moving traffic, already thousands of feet away from danger.

Blake looked to the masked people beside them, but each sat in a combat ready position, waiting for the next move. None seemed ready to talk.

"Who are you people?" Blake asked.

One of them looked down to Blake, who was still crouched on the metal floor. "We're not to give any information until—"

"You're HALO, aren't you?" Roger cut in. As soon as the words entered the air, Blake could see the man's eyes behind the mask relax.

"Yes. We are."

13

The night sky was always lit in the upper districts. The bright lights from the skyscrapers would always give off a bright fluorescent hue that seemed to reach far beyond the peaks of the buildings. There were some that said standing in the city center at night felt no different from day.

And Jon Reegan stood above it all.

From his penthouse apartment at the top of Reegan United's central offices, for this moment and many like it, Jon remained the person highest above the city, seeing the bright lights shimmering below him.

He would often look to this view in the dark—the overhead natural lighting of his penthouse turned completely off. Standing here, behind just two inches of glass from a three thousand foot drop, the noise and chaos of the company could dissipate. He had always found these moments of solitude to be the most important—action taken after days of hard work would weaken him. Even the best of athletes relies on their downtime just as much as their training to become the best in the world.

So Reegan had ordered his penthouse apartment be off limits to any technological advances that he himself had been so influential in creating. No phones littered the walls, and no view screens could be seen within these walls. Even the doors were analog—reliant on deadbolts and keys versus the automatic doors of the rest of the office. There were strict orders to keep as much of Reegan United away from this space as possible. But tonight, not even the solitude could prove to be enough for Reegan.

Earlier on this day, a breach occurred.

To be clear: breaches *never* occurred. Not once in the decades-long history of Reegan United and it's Replicant Services division had a single person crossed over successfully. Attempts? Surely. Many crazed lunatics had to be put down in order to secure a proper bridge between worlds. Not a single life given by lunatic or officer had been in vain—not to Reegan. No, looking out tonight at this sky, seeing this empire before him? It had all been worth it. It had *always* been worth it.

So tonight, Reegan was awaiting something rather unusual—a report. Luckily enough for him, the surveillance installed throughout the city served its purpose beautifully.

"Blake," Reegan said out loud, to the city itself. "Roger." The names of the first two to commit a breach. They had succeeded in one thing—infamy. Reegan had already ensured that anyone responsible for the breach, on both sides of the breached Terminus, had been thoroughly dealt with. The infrastructure was already in the process of being altered to accommodate the new weaknesses revealed in the system, and heads had already rolled. Reegan had built this world on efficiency, progress, but ultimately, pragmatism. There was nothing that would be left to chance, and given into in face of empathy.

"Sir," the voice of his assistant came over the intercom—the only sign of technology within the room. "The officer is here to see you."

Reegan moved to his desk, where a single button sat, standing out against the wood. He pressed it down. "Send him in." He said in a quiet tone, and moved back to his view.

Entering the room soon would be the commanding officer of the militia of the twelfth district—the one containing the breach. And while Blake and Roger had gone south into the sixteenth, this particular officer was fully in charge of today's search. As predicted, the men had been careless in their escape from the decoy building, and left a pile of DNA evidence for Reegan to access. The only thing that could make this particular day any better, was a report of the full termination of both men.

Unfortunately for Reegan, the officer entered the room and offered far less encouraging news.

"Blake and Roger were intercepted by HALO before we could get to them," the officer said, choosing not to mince words. "We're working on a current location—"

Reegan raised a hand, silencing the officer. "You're telling me you don't have a location?"

"HALO's using one of our vehicles," the officer explained. "A stolen anti-surveillance van. We're talking to the designers to find a workaround, but they're moving fast, and the vehicle is ironclad."

"Please tell me you've got the DNA sorted."

The officer handed Reegan a manila envelope containing the desired information. "It's all in here. We've had enough DNA from the hotel room to scan them against our registries. Although the results are…surprising to say the least."

"Track down any of their alternates," Reegan said, setting the envelope down on a desk. "Pull them from cold storage if they're on ice. We might need them."

"Alternates?" the officer asked. "Sir, I don't understand."

"You're about to learn a great deal about how our society operates," Reegan said calmly. He didn't like briefing even his closest aides on the subject of the truth about the work of RDS. Most even operating the trafficking itself knew very little about the truth. But there was no avoiding this. Not for this officer. "My assistant will brief you shortly."

"Yes, sir," the officer stated. "And if their loss means I'm no longer handling this case—"

"Oh, no, officer," Reegan interrupted. "These men escaped from your district. The most exhaustively covered district in our entire province, save for this one we're in now. This is your problem. I expect you'll fix this issue?"

The officer took a moment to respond. "Of course, sir."

"My assistant will also give you the necessary recourses. You'll have unlimited access to our entire network, as well as our special forces to be deployed as you see fit. I hope that you'll utilize it wisely."

The officer left the room without another word, leaving Reegan back to his quiet view.

He had no doubt that this particular officer would fail him. No officer had ever been trained to deal with a breach— by vary nature, officers had no knowledge of such things. Only the special forces unit, a band of just twelve men, would know about the truth. That was, on *this* side of the world.

Reegan moved back over to his intercom. "What time is it currently in America, Eastern Standard?" He asked. Within seconds, his assistant had a response: "Just past six in the morning, sir."

"Prepare our Terminus for immediate operation," he said. "I'm going to have to pay a few people a visit."

Reegan took one last enjoyment of his quiet penthouse, before moving forward towards the door.

This wasn't going to be left to one officer, or even the special forces unit. A breach threatened the very existence not only of this empire, but the carefully crafted ignorance of those existing parallel to this world. His partners that resided in that alternate world had to know just how severe this breach was, and just how compromising it could prove to be.

Reegan was going to pay a few incapable people a *very* memorable visit.

14

HALO had been keeping Blake and Roger locked away in some holding facility, far out of town. Blake and Roger had ridden in the back of an armored truck for what felt like hours, and before that had been handcuffed out of 'precaution' and led into a maze of darkened rooms. The little glimpse of the outside world Blake was able to see between the truck and the facility had shown him that the massive skyscrapers that had defined the center of the city were far away. Out here, there seemed to be nothing but red dirt, rocks, and clay.

Inside the cell where Blake and Roger had spent the past two days, the two had grown acclimated to a routine. Food was delivered in the same fashion as meals to prisoners in solitary confinement—through a small, sealable hole, and without a word exchanged between them. A bathroom was built into one of the far corners, complete with a curtain for privacy.

The cell felt more like a cheap studio apartment than a prison otherwise. The two were granted clean clothes in their sizes, as well as comfortable beds for the two of them. A couch was also in the room, but little in terms of entertainment was provided. It was nice not to have to dig into their rations, but this HALO organization that Tamara had suggested they look out for was turning out, so far, to be elusive, distant, and not too much better than where they had found themselves before.

Sometime on the second day, Roger expressed that concern. "Two days in here and nothing from any of the guys that kidnapped us. This doesn't seem any better than running from the police."

"They were shooting to kill," Blake said, feeling the need to defend their hosts. "If HALO hadn't have found us when they did, there's a good chance we'd be dead by now."

"Maybe they're just prolonging that possibility," Roger said. "Maybe they're just holding us until they can trade us back to whoever wants us dead."

"Tamara is probably captured or dead at this point," Blake pointed out. "There is no reason she'd do that for HALO or any other organization just for hostages alone."

Before they could discuss the fact any further, a loud buzz shook both of them from their positions. The red, metal door on the far wall creaked open to reveal several men in tactical suits waiting in the hall.

"Come with us," one of the men said, stepping forward. Judging by the green band on his left-side jacket, he was in charge of the other men. Blake also recognized him as the same man that had rescued them earlier from the city's police force.

"Where to?" Roger asked as he stood up. Blake tried to shoot him a warning glance, but the man responded before either of them could say another word:

"You're meeting with leadership," the man continued. "There was a delay."

"Sure," Roger said, laced with sarcasm. He walked out of the door, leaving Blake to trail behind. The two moved into the center of the armed escort, and the group moved collectively away from the room. If anything, Blake was glad to finally be out of there.

The hallways here had a distinct underground feeling to them, not unlike the complex back north of Ithaca that had led them this far. The walls radiated a cool air, and the hallways grew shorter and damper with each step downward. Different splits in the path here led down dozens of different locations and possibilities, ensuring that even if the two were able to get away from the armed men, they would be hopelessly lost in the massive labyrinth.

They paused outside a door at the end of one of the hallways, waiting for the leading man to knock on the door. It opened without much hesitation, and the armed men split down the middle, clearing a path for the two to enter the room. Without needing any further explanation, the two entered the room, hearing the door slam shut behind them. The leading man had followed them inside, and waited at the door.

Inside, several men and women stood at a circular table near the center of the room, lit only by an artificial sunlight above them. Alongside the walls, several others worked away at view screens and translucent glass like the ones Blake had seen in the convenience store. The entire room was roughly the side of a small restaurant, and appeared to be a base of operations. At the head of the table, a woman dressed in a distinct dark green pantsuit, as opposed to the black worn by other occupants of the room. She gestured forward to two open seats in front of her.

"Please," she said with a smile. "Have a seat."

Blake and Roger took hesitant steps forward, sitting down at the table. As they did, each of the other men and women in black sat as well, leaving the leader standing by herself.

"As our friend here has said, or so I hope," she said, looking to the man who had escorted the two into the room, "we do apologize about the delay. Many wheels are in motion that have to be attended to."

"Being kept in the dark hasn't helped us understand what you're trying to accomplish here," Blake said. His initial observation of the room had faded away, and now he sought nothing but answers. "No one has told us a word about who you are since we were captured."

"Captured?" she asked. "As I was told, you entered into our custody under your own accord. We don't capture people such as yourselves. In fact, we were hoping to know why you were so willing to travel with us."

"There was this woman," Roger said. "Someone who led here. Helped us cross over. Tamara. She told us to find HALO."

A silence drew across the room first at the mention of Tamara, then faint chatter seemed to arise in little bursts. The woman raised her hand, silencing the discussion. "Tamara is one of our own. What became of her?"

"We don't know," Blake said. "She opened this...Terminus, as she called it, to help us get here. We were ambushed as the last minute. She's most likely been captured by whoever runs this province."

Another trickle of murmurs, before the woman spoke again: "Tamara held a very key position in the men who were trying to stop you. She worked for them, but for us first. She was a mole that passed information through your world into our own. The fact that she sacrificed herself for you makes us very curious as to why such a thing has occurred." She paused for a moment, then loosened. "We've started out on the wrong foot, surely. My name is Audrey Chamberlain. Chief Commander of HALO. The man who escorted you inside is First Officer Everett Goodwin. He's in charge of operations in the most central districts of our province ."

"And what operations exactly does that entail?" Blake asked.

"HALO operates much like freedom fighters do in your world, Blake," Chamberlain explained. "We work against Reegan United and its autocracy in order to bring peace and justice to both of our worlds. And I believe you'll find that working with us will be in your best interest."

"I've read about your organization already," Roger said. "You're classified as a terrorist group."

"Reegan United has complete control over the national bank, infrastructure, and the military," Everett explained. He stepped forward from his place beside the door and approached the table. "The integrated system of technology in the city hub is nothing short of full-proof for them. Every step taken, every transaction held, is all recorded and stored in massive data mines just outside of the city. They've accomplished this over decades of taking advantage of our corrupt political system and undermining the people that placed us here. HALO started out as a peaceful party opposed to the dominance of Reegan United. Over time, they've out casted us as terrorists and make working in the public eye impossible."

"Tell us," Chamberlain said. "Why are you here?"

"It's simple. Somebody from this world, somehow, has taken people from us," Blake said. "I don't know how many people were taken. Maybe tens, maybe hundreds, maybe thousands. But among those included my wife, and Roger's sister. We came to this world to find them."

A few looks were exchanged between the men and women in the group before Chamberlain spoke again. "You've both discovered a truth you'll soon learn that few know. The connection between our worlds is only decades old, and that secret has been a national security issue for both your world and ours. We've come to learn this truth at the expense of many lives. The only difference is that your world loses, and ours gains."

"What exactly do you gain?" Roger said, his voice raising. "Why take the people from us? Why is our world comfortable with letting this happen?"

"Why is your world alright with the purchasing of animals?" Everett asked. "It's the same to Reegan United, in their own sadistic ways. They pay heavily to your United States, in exchange for assistance in hiding the truth. They profit as well from the civilians on this side that don't know any better, and purchase the stolen people like slaves."

"Our society is more utopian than your own," Chamberlain explained. "We've solved many of the issues you currently are still battling. Our world has advanced healthcare. Poverty is lowering day by day. Assistance and help are always easily attainable, and the average citizen is wealthier than ever. Eventually, our abilities to fix problems began to bottom out. And eventually, there was something we couldn't buy our way out of."

"Death," Blake said. He was beginning to realize.

"Exactly," Chamberlain continued. "Reegan United was beginning to take over, and its origins in scientific exploration led them to a discovery that could have changed the nature of our world as we knew it. The first Terminus was built during this time—a bridge between worlds. A device powerful enough to deny physic, space, and time. I believe quantum mechanics is one way of phrasing it, where you are from. Instead of the grand opportunity it presented for our worlds to collide, Jon Reegan decided to take matters into his own hands."

"Once it was discovered that each person in our world had a duplicate counterpart in yours," Everett said, "than it was all too easy to consider the possibility of human trafficking. Reegan United had made great advancements in genetic cloning, and decided to take those from your world and sell them off as 'duplicates' of loved ones."

"Replace your own family members," Roger thought out loud. "My god."

"How did they not realize these were other people from another world?" Blake asked.

"Their push for surveillance gave them unprecedented access to civilians, much like how advertisers work in your world," Chamberlain explained. "However, Reegan United has far more access than your world could even dream of. By scanning every facet of a person's life—their internet histories, their physical habits, their purchases, their actions—they could create an artificial memory that was close enough to the real person."

"So began Reegan Duplicate Services," Everett continued. "RDS. For quite a high price, you could replace your lost loved ones within weeks, and move forward as if nothing had ever happened. They would have just enough similarities and remember enough of the lives of the one that they replaced in order for people to be comfortable purchasing them. And the idea that they're clones makes it far more comfortable for them than the reality of stealing from another world. Cloning technology sounds far more feasible than inter-dimensional travel."

"There's billions of people in our world," Blake said. "How could they possibly track down each person?"

"The national registry," Chamberlain said. "Reegan United has more than enough information on civilians in this world, including their DNA. They use that information in conjunction with the vast recourses of your world to track down purchased people, and they're getting more and more efficient every day. Simply find the selection of candidates, see if the DNA matches—"

"And take them."

"Exactly."

Blake's mind raced to assemble a counterargument—something to prove to these people that they were baseless and wrong. But it all made sense—from the military complex back in Ithaca, to the world he had seen outside of HALO's walls. The very idea of this concept a week ago would have been enough to cause Blake to laugh if the face of anyone who suggested it.

And now, it was all too real.

15

Blake and Roger were granted full access to the HALO facilities after meeting with Commander Chamberlain. They remained in their single-room quarters, but could now roam the vast underground lair of HALO, including access to the cafeteria, and information from the digital archives within the complex. However, any internet access was strictly forbidden, as Reegan United could easily trace the location of the two men.

The rest of their meeting was spent answering question after question from each member of that table. From their origins to their meeting together, Blake and Roger explained all that they could to the men and women. They seemed impressed with Blake's field knowledge and Roger's expertise with technology, but offered no further course of action—instead, recessing and informing them that, at a later date, they'd be contacted as to what HALO's wishes were for them. For all the information they were provided, the secrecy quickly returned, and Blake and Roger were back to silent faces and lingering eyes from each corner of the complex.

The two of them reacted to the full news of their situation in different ways. Roger seemed much more talkative than Blake—droning on and on about the logistical nightmare it would be to index all of the data on each individual person. He spent much of his time in the archives, learning and studying the algorithms that had made this place a reality. And sometimes, Blake would visit him there, just long enough to ask if there had been more information available about the outside world. Once he learned there would rarely ever be access, he soon stopped asking.

As for Blake, he kept to himself, mostly. He had figured that Roger's more comfortable stance on the situation came from his access to information—something Roger seemed to value more than his loss, which occurred decades ago. The memories of Casey still haunted Blake far stronger. The satisfaction that she was alive was replaced with the fear that her mind had been permanently taken from her. Anytime he tried to ask the specifics of how Reegan United was able to do this, he wasn't given any answers. Nor could anyone comfort him in knowing whether or not the process was reversible.

Still, it was not all to say Roger did not care about finding his sister. Both of them spent the evenings discussing when they would finally be free to leave the complex, talk to Chamberlain again and see about their original mission to find their loved ones. And as the days continued, Blake felt more like he hadn't really been freed, but rather given a larger cage to play in.

Sometime near day seven of their pseudo-entrapment, Blake found himself perched against the railing of a raised catwalk. Here, the hallway had to stretch above a large section of empty cave, and Blake could see the sheer drop of several dozen feet downward, into the underground waterfall and certainly to rather painful death. It was this closeness to death that Blake found so strange that they had allowed in HALO's facilities. It was as if it remained a constant reminder for what lay on the other side of these walls.

"This whole facility used to be Reegan's, you know."

Blake turned his head to see Everett approaching, out of uniform. The younger man looked strange in such casual clothes—his sharp features highlighting the unkempt nature of his standard issue shirt and cargo shorts. He wore with him as well a more familiar face, as the two had crossed paths more than once within the halls.

"It looks a lot like the complex we broke into to get here," Blake noted, looking to the walls of the cave. "There was this massive facility they had built underground for their Terminus. It seemed like they could move thousands through that place."

"They planned ahead," Everett explained. "We estimate the number of stolen over the years to be in the hundreds, not the thousands. The facilities like this were built originally for a far more active transportation hub. The truth is, purchasing a person, whether or not they are a clone, is still much too expensive for anyone normal to purchase."

"So why run the company?" Blake asked. "Why operate something on that scale when the logistics alone would eat up any profits?"

"No one really knows," Everett admitted. "Jon Reegan seems to operate on the principle of it all rather than for money. And when you're in his position, with all the money and power in the world, perhaps robbing from the next world seems like a hobby."

"What a fucked-up hobby."

"Which is why we're trying to stop him," Everett said, "and anyone willing to support his system. Taking down the duplicate operation he runs is just one small step in the right direction. If we can reveal the truth to the general public, we could garner enough support to begin dismantling his empire and returning our world to the way things used to be. So far, we've been limited to stealing facilities such as this one in districts sympathetic to our cause, far enough away from the grid as to be forgotten. We mask our digital signatures so that, in the eyes of Jon Reegan, this is just one of many abandoned buildings on the outside of his empire."

"I heard in the news in town that you guys had captured another one of these facilities," Blake mentioned.

"Which was why we were busy when you first arrived," Everett said. "We've been looking for a key to solving this puzzle. A way to get the upper hand against him."

"And you're waiting to see what can be done with me and Roger," Blake said.

"Possibly. It's a complicated situation."

"You don't have to bullshit with me, Officer," Blake said. "I'm a Marine, and back where I'm from, that means I've been in some seriously complicated situations. Having me and Roger—people that this Reegan fellow wants so badly—as ammo for a negotiated trade, would be something I'd easily consider."

"We're looking at all of our options, Blake," Everett admitted. "And as a military man, I'm sure you can respect that."

The two didn't talk much for a moment after that, instead opting to look out to the origin of the waterfall-a hole in the cave walls that, no doubt, led to the outside world.

"We're tired of hiding," Everett said. "We live under the ground like roaches, most of the time. If there's a way for us to move forward, we'll do it. And you know, you're the first of your kind to cross through a Terminus. Most people from your world are killed before they ever get so far. So don't think we don't acknowledge your potential."

"Well, I'm certainly flattered."

Everett stepped away from Blake soon after this—perhaps he had sensed that debating someone so driven would lead him nowhere. Before he left the cave, he offered Blake one last piece of advice: "I've seen your record, Blake. HALO would be crazy to pass up that sort of opportunity in someone. Just give it time."

And with that, he left.

***

Blake waited in his and Roger's holding room for quite some time before Roger appeared again. He had spent the majority of his day in the archives, while Blake had been in the middle of a long set of body weight exercises to pass the time.

"Any way I could convince you to check out the archives tomorrow?" Roger asked as he dug through his backpack. He produced a personal item he had insisted on bringing—his personal journal. He scrawled in it wildly each night, hoping never to forget the information he had learned. "There's a wealth of information there. It's incredible how much dirt there is on anyone. It's as if these people exist more online than off."

"It makes no difference if they decide to turn us over," Blake said. He was laying on the ground, counting the seconds before his next set. "What use is information to a dead man?"

"Chamberlain said these things take time," Roger countered. "There's not much else we can do."

Blake sat up from the look and looked over to his partner. "There's nothing on that information I asked you about?"

Roger gave a stark look, before rising and slowly closing the door between the room and the outer headquarters of HALO. "Not a thing. I've compared the layout of this facility to the few blueprints in the archives, but nothing comes close. And I'd rather stop looking. I don't know how well they can monitor our actions, internet surveillance or not."

Blake let out a frustrated sigh. Waiting was not part of Blake's abilities. He was a man of action—someone that would easily break out of this facility as soon as he could. But he was also a man of reason, and knew escaping was impossible without a blueprint of the facilities and knowing just how far they could go. Quietly, he and Roger had been looking to see if it was even a possibility, and that chance was quickly becoming exhausted. But it was becoming increasingly clear that, even with Blake's training, this place was almost impossible to escape from.

Roger continued on, not waiting for a response from Blake: "There's no real way of discovering where we are spatially. We couldn't figure out how far we drove to get here, nevertheless come to terms with how fast we were going. The doors here are biometrical. Any access has to come from the mainframe or someone with an approved bio-code. There's no ports to access, no way forward...we're not getting out of here unless they let us. And I think you've known that this whole time."

"I wasn't going to give up," Blake said. "I'm *not* going to give up. We have to access all our options, same as them."

"Then why don't you do the smart thing and figure this stuff out with me?" Roger asked. "If there's any information in the archives that could help us, we need it. And yeah—there's nothing on escaping here, sure. But when we first got here, we didn't know what the hell we were doing. Now we can. This place is incredible—"

"I'm not interested in this place, Roger," Blake said. "I'm interested in finding my wife."

Roger lowered his head, and the two didn't speak much after that. Blake finished the rest of his exercises and took a shower. He was about to climb into bed when he watched Roger open his bag again, and pull out a small, leather-bound book.

"What's that?" Blake asked.

"My father's journal," Roger said. He cracked open the yellowed pages. "I picked up the habit from him. Losing my sister was hard on me, sure, but I was very young. I could've easily moved past it. But my father? It consumed him for the rest of his life. He wrote down every lead, and every possibility he could think of. He's even got little mementos of her stuffed away in here. I guess I picked up the search for Sam more for him than me. I had to watch my parents fall apart the rest of their lives. Torn by what they could have done to prevent what happened."

Roger felt a specific page, before reading it: "'February 8th, 1978. Roger and Patricia went back to Central Park today. I wish they wouldn't tell me about these things. My new office is on the other side of the park. I've taken to the subway more often down. The less I have to see of that place, the better. Inside, I see my daughter around every corner. I hear her in every child's voice. And each time I see my son, I know he was never supposed to be an only child.'"

"I want to see my sister again," Roger explained. "I've never stopped wanting that. If I can get closure for Dad, maybe that would be enough."

Blake thought for a moment. "Yeah," he finally breathed out. "Maybe."

"It seems like your loss didn't do much for your own relationships, either," Roger joked. He gently set the journal down on the table and leaned back. "From what you described, you and Dustin aren't exactly the best of friends."

"We used to be," Blake laughed. The dark humor was quickly replaced by the realization of what really happened to them. "God, we used to be," he repeated. "Dustin had my back in more than one situation. And when shit got real—when one of our own men decided to risk the lives of innocents for his own sick gain—he was the only one on my side."

"Christ," Roger said. "Sounds like an asshole."

Blake's mind rushed to Jordan. "Fighting broke him. And it almost broke me."

Before Roger could respond, a knock on the door jolted the both of them from their conversations. The door opened to reveal Everett.

"Guys," he started. "It's time."

16

Blake and Roger were once again led down a familiar path through the headquarters and brought into the main operations room of HALO. This time, however, it was only Commander Chamberlain and Everett in the room.

Blake didn't even bother to take a seat. "Go ahead, Commander."

Chamberlain stood, poised and sharp, in stance and in speech. "We're more than aware of your ideas to escape our facilities, Mr. Collier. Did you not think we'd be monitoring your actions?"

"Honestly, Commander, I don't care that you knew," Blake said. He could feel Roger squirming beside him, but paid it no mind. People like Chamberlain were people he was familiar with. Apologizing would look twice as bad as getting caught ever did. "If it was in your best interest to hand us over to Reegan's men, you were more than careful enough not to leave us able to discover any secrets. There was a slight chance of gaining the upper hand, and we looked into it. I see nothing wrong with that."

The Commander's face was unreadable. "You're both the most wanted men in the entire province, you know. Reegan's got your face plastered on every view screen and every wall he could find. The reward for your capture is so astronomical, I had to consider my options. I see nothing wrong with that, either."

The conversation faded to an indeterminate halt, and neither party seemed to back down. As with everything with HALO that Blake had discovered, this was a test. His conversation earlier with Everett had also been a test. Every file and every page Roger had discovered was a test. A test with no clear answers.

But as luck would have it, they must have done something right, as Chamberlain relaxed in front of them. "However, you provide a service that no amount of money ever could. Reegan's desire to find you clearly consumes him. The desperation and the speed at which he released his men to capture you in the city showed flaws in his strategy. And in that desperation, we were able to rescue you. If Reegan were to come close to capturing you again, we'd have far more of a chance to discover a pathway to dismantling his empire. Officer?"

Everett stepped forward. "Just before the two of you arrived through the Terminus, HALO launched a covert operation into one of Reegan's Duplicate complexes. Most of these are fronts for a paper trail, leading nowhere near any definitive proof that we need. But this time was different. Inside, we were able to stage a failed attempt at hacking into Reegan's internal network. Reegan thinks we failed, and in many ways, we did. Many died on that night to ensure the plan was executed precisely."

"Because he thought he had failed," Chamberlain explained, "he didn't bother to dismantle the access terminals that lay within the building. And luckily for us, we were able to…convince one of the technical engineers to work alongside us, from the inside. We now have full access to the DNA directory, as well as footage, live and recorded, from all districts within the province. We've gained an upper hand and he doesn't even know it."

"The raid on the RDS compound," Blake remembered. "I saw that on the news back in the city."

"Reegan's been smart enough to bury the information that could connect him to the seriousness of his crimes," Everett said. "All of the Terminus locations are decentralized, and as soon as we can capture a location, his men are quick to shut it down remotely. We don't have the manpower to take on Reegan directly, but if we can find the center of operations—"

"You'd be able to shut it down from the inside," Blake concluded. "You'd move in like a parasite and be able to dismantle him before he even realized you were there."

"It's our best option of destabilizing his power," Chamberlain said. "If we can get discernible proof out here to the right people, there's still a chance for us to radically change things for the better. But we need your help."

"You want us to be bait for what's essentially a dictator?" Roger asked. "You said his desperation in capturing us is leaving windows of opportunity for yourselves."

"You won't be bait," Everett explained. "You'll be under our full protection at all times. Just a few public appearances at strategic locations will be enough for us to map out the infrastructure we're working against. He'll be forced to unveil his depositories and secret hideaways throughout the city. The digital archives show us public places, but not private. With your help, we can access both."

"Then we're going to have to make a deal," Blake said, "because I didn't come to help on some grand mission for your sake. I came for my wife."

Chamberlain and Everett exchanged a look, signaling Everett to produce a translucent tablet from the table. Turning it on, Everett revealed a long list of codes and numbers to the two men. "Using the DNA archives, we can pinpoint the exact location of your loved ones. In exchange for helping us, we will help you find them."

"My sister's been missing for decades," Roger said. "I don't have any DNA."

"I don't either," Blake added. "It's not something we tend to keep where I'm from."

"Do you know when your wife went missing?" Chamberlain asked.

"Of course," Blake replied. "To the day."

"Do you have a photo?"

Blake grimaced. "Tamara had us leave them for fear of tracking us. Any photos I had would have been in there."

"Then we'll compare the time of DNA entries to your physical description of your wife, along with the surveillance footage of that day in front of the same building you both arrived in," Everett explained. "It should take no more than a few days."

"As for your sister," Chamberlain said to Roger, "unfortunately, without a current physical description or DNA, it's going to be much more difficult."

"We're twins," Roger said. "Take my DNA and run it through your program."

"You're *paternal* twins," Everett said. "I'm afraid the DNA won't align. Not enough for a precise match. Even something so close as yourself won't be enough."

The room went quiet again for a moment, and Blake couldn't help but feel terrible for Roger. He had come so far to fulfill something for himself—for his father, even—and to be told this far in that finding his sister might be impossible, was cruel. He watched as his newfound friend seemed to lower his head in thought. For all the work he and his father had put into this, for all the journals written—

"Wait," Blake said, snapping the attention in the room back to him. He looked to Roger. "The journal. You said your father kept mementos of your sister in that journal."

"Yeah?" Roger asked.

"Is there any sort of clothing, or toy in there? Anything that would have DNA?"

Roger's eyes begin to light up. "Maybe."

With that, he turned in place, and made straight for the door. Blake followed after him, moving quickly through the hallways that connected them to their quarters. They ran past several of the guards, much to their own dismay, and Blake could hear the footsteps of Everett close behind him. It was another long minute of running before the group arrived in their quarters, where Blake arrived to see a frantic Roger, flipping through the pages of his father's journal.

"Here, here!" He exclaimed, producing a small red strand of fabric from the journal—a ribbon. He pushed it to Everett, who examined the small blonde strand, holding it up to the light.

"The hair root is still attached," he said. "This could be enough. I'll get it down to the lab immediately."

Everett left the room, leaving Blake and Roger alone to catch their breath. And in that moment, Blake could see Roger look over to him, and for the first time since their arrival, give out a chuckle and a smile.

And in this moment, things seemed better than ever.

***

Sam's hair strand, left inside Roger's father's journal, was the perfect specimen for HALO's lab to extract DNA from. Everett was able to run the DNA code information against the database and found a perfect match—a woman in one of the outer districts, away from the prying eyes of the surveillance footage, but still registered with an address to her name.

"The DNA registry has been exhaustive for Reegan," Everett had explained to him in a briefing that took place later that day. "He's not short on resources, but his weakness has always been time. It'll be another few years before he has the capability to track motion in every corner of the province. Once he does...there won't be much hope for keeping places like this hidden."

The following day was spent preparing for the long journey northward. The province was a massive city—spreading from the center districts and clawing outward in all directions. HALO was hidden away in a southwestern district, near the border, while Sam was located thousands of miles northward, near an ocean. HALO could only afford to send so many men with them, so Everett nominated himself and a team of hand-chosen partners to accompany Blake and Roger on the trip.

In total, the group had been afforded one of the anti-surveillance vans, food and supplies, as well as significant firepower. And for good reason.

"There's a stronghold here," Chamberlain explained the night before the journey, pointing to a map of the province. The stronghold was right in between the HALO headquarters and the northern district. "There's no convenient way around here, and any travel within a hundred miles will be filled with roadblocks. Since you two became fugitives, that radius had most likely doubled. I'd be surprised if you made it through unscathed."

"We can't go around?" Roger asked.

"That trip would take far too long," Chamberlain explained. Any more eastward, and you cross into the city center, where surveillance would surely catch you. Any more westward, and you reach an impassable mountain range. We'll be able to remotely move you past many of the roadblocks, but I doubt we can avoid them all."

"We'll handle whatever comes our way," Blake said. "Any progress on finding Casey?"

"Not so far," Chamberlain sighed. Since their initial meeting, Blake had given every detail of Casey's physique to HALO. They had been crawling through surveillance footage the entire week after her disappearance from Blake's world, but the number of women matching the descriptions in the location of the Terminus were in the thousands. "We'll get you a photoset soon."

Blake nodded. "What about these roadblocks? If Reegan is trying to capture us, don't we need to make a big impression?"

"Not here," Everett said. "We know this western stronghold well. He's not going to have his base of operations here. The manpower is too great for us to risk you two getting captured. The best course of action is to lay low. Once we narrow down his possible bases, we'll have a better chance of carefully exposing you."

"Alright then," Blake said. "Let's get moving."

Early the next morning, Blake and Roger were taken further into the headquarters than they had ever been before this moment. They were taken with their new entourage to an underground holding bay. Inside, the entire arsenal of HALO could be found—a motley crew of vehicles, and even a few airplanes as well. HALO was formidable enough to poke holes in Reegan's abilities, sure, but a direct attack would surely fail. It would be hundreds versus hundreds of thousands—a sheer impossibility.

Chamberlain accompanied them downward to the bay, and seemed confident in their mission. "We'll be in touch at all times," she said. "Move quickly. The slower the pace, the easier it'll be for Reegan to figure out your location. You may not know it yet, but he'll do whatever he can to prevent us from finding the base of his human trafficking operation."

"Whoever he is," Blake said, "I've fought worse. We'll handle it."

With that, Blake entered the vehicle, and sat beside his new traveling companions. If anything, he was finally glad to be away from the HALO facility, as the car traveled upwards and back above ground.

The road ahead led to Roger's sister, Reegan's men, but most importantly, to Casey.

17

"Sir?"

Jon Reegan turned from his view screen to see his assistant standing at the edge of the doorway.

"It's time."

Reegan's quarters in this world were usually much more quaint—on paper, he shouldn't even exist here. Today found him in a small luxury hotel room, three floors below the ground level. Very few people would ever enter this room, and fewer still ever came back out.

Reegan and his assistant moved—escorted by a few of his own men—up three flights of stairs and into the main atrium of the building. They moved to the loading area just outside, and moved into the single SUV waiting for them. The car rolled the moment the doors closed, right on schedule, and into the Manhattan streets.

He had spent the past several days in Manhattan— working with contacts within the United States government. There had been quite a few angry phone conversations, weak leaders, and meek responses to his simple question: how did they plan to help stop Blake?

Eventually, it became evident that Reegan was going to have to handle much of this with his own assets. Contacts in this world were inefficient as best—and utterly incapable at worst. They worked with outdated and archaic technology, even with access to Reegan's own advancements. They were slowed down by bureaucracy, democracy, or just plain resolve. It wasn't a way to operate a proper partnership, and Reegan felt as if these people didn't understand the danger Blake had placed them all in. All they seemed to understand were the paychecks Reegan provided.

The SUV pulled into the back entrance of the Lieutenant Governor's Office just east of Midtown—a modest little building, dwarfed by even its closest neighbors. As planned, several of the Governor's personal armed men escorted them discretely inside, and the entourage moved into a back waiting room, where the Lieutenant Governor was waiting to greet them.

"Good Morning," the man smiled. The wispy hairs on the top of his head signaled a male-pattern baldness that refused to be accepted. This man wasn't important to impress in the slightest, and Reegan treated him as such.

"Do you have him?"

The Lieutenant Governor nodded, his smile fading. He pointed to a closet nearby. "He's in there. Did you want to see him—"

"That's fine, thank you," Reegan said. "Do let the Governor know I'm ready to begin."

The Lieutenant Governor seemed confused by Reegan's actions, but left the room on cue.

As the group waited for the Governor to arrive, Reegan had his men quickly re-assemble the room for their needs. The conference table in the center of the room was propped up against one of the bare walls, and the chairs stacked beside them. This left a clear line of sight between Reegan and where his guests would be standing. Behind him, heavy breathing could be heard from the closet door, but he paid it no mind. Soon enough, he would be put to good use. Reegan's men left soon afterward, preparing to bring in the guests. And for a moment, all was quiet.

"Mr. Reegan," came the Governor as he entered the room, taking his spot beside Reegan. He talked to Reegan as a child would to a parent on edge. "I hope everything's gone smoothly so far."

"As smooth as it could have gone," Reegan mentioned in passing. "We wouldn't be handling this at all if it wasn't for the failure of your men to protect our assets in Ithaca."

The Governor tried to minimize his failures: "Our government here is divided between state and national, as you know. My men weren't at the complex—"

"Sure, but they *were* aware of Roger Kerns, as well as Blake Collier's investigation into these matters. Or does your own police force handle nothing in this state?"

The Governor didn't speak. Perhaps he feared losing the considerable fortune Reegan was providing for him. He *should* have been fearing a far worse punishment.

"We'll fix this problem, I assure you," Reegan continued for him. "And quickly, once we convince these men of the severity of the situation."

"Many of these men are decorated veterans," the Governor protested. "And loyal as well. I'm not quite sure if they'll agree to these terms."

"We'll see about that."

The door opened, and several men entered the room, single file, and led by Reegan's men. They had been brought here under what had been told to them as 'difficult circumstances,' and Reegan made sure they were in civilian clothing. The men seemed a bit surprised to see the Governor of their state standing next to a cordial, clean-cut man such as Reegan. They stood as if they were on a police line, and faced the two men. By the door, one of Reegan's men waited for his cue.

"Good morning, gentleman," the Governor started. "We hate to bring you in on such short notice—"

"Let's spare the pleasantries, please," Reegan interrupted. The Governor backed down, knowing his place. "You men have been brought here together because you all spent considerable time with a Blake Collier, is that correct?"

No response.

"Blake Collier has become a fugitive. Driven mad by the loss of his wife, he's resorted to drastic measures to find her. He's been convinced by a conspiracist that some other world beyond this exists, and that somewhere in that world, he may find her. Now, some of you may or may not have heard his theories and stories. Some of you may have been asked rather *politely* by your superiors to keep Blake off the scent. And most of you knew when it was best to keep your mouth shut about this matter."

Again, there was no response from the men. Just hard faces, and blank stares.

"Well, I'm here to tell you that he was right, and despite our best efforts, we cannot find him. That is where you come in. I'll keep it short: you're going to accompany me back to where I'm from. You're going to work with *my* men to find *your* man. And if he's lucky, he just might make it out of this alive. Who knows? Maybe he'd surrender to you."

"Returning Blake and his newfound friend home is our top priority," the Governor said, trying to add to the conversation. "It's best for us all is he come home safely."

"And why should we help you?" one of the Marines said—unintimidated.

"Well, it's pretty simple," Reegan started. "You might have noticed that one of your former squad mates isn't here." He turned around, and opened the closet door.

Out of the door, Dustin Barnes collapsed with a heap onto the carpet. His face was a brutal mixture of red and brown—his eyes held shut as to keep his bleeding head from pouring into them. He was gagged and handcuffed, as well as tied together at the ankles. Out of all of the things the

Marines had heard from Reegan, this seemed to be the first to really affect them.

"Sergeant Barnes here was given some very simple instructions," Reegan said. "Don't talk to Blake. And because he did, he is responsible for dragging you all into this situation. He failed us. And I don't appreciate failure. Especially when it jeopardizes not only the affairs of this country, but mine as well."

Reegan stepped forward, signaling his man by the door. He stepped forward, producing a silver pistol for Reegan to grab. Reegan moved next to the single Marine that had talked so far, and offered the pistol to him.

"Would you like to execute this man for treason?" he asked the Marine.

The man didn't even look to the weapon. "We don't pass sentences here."

"Your decision," Reegan said. He signaled to his man again, who moved to Dustin, lifted him from the ground, and carried him out of the room. Reegan was actually rather satisfied by this turn of events—a live man was more of an asset than a dead one.

"So you'll join me?"

None of the men budged at his words. Reegan could feel their hatred through their eyes as they glared to him. These bunch were harder than he had given them credit for. More incentive was needed.

Reegan fiddled with the weapon that still remained in his hands. "How many men am I going to have to shoot before I get at least one of you to agree to my terms?"

No response.

Reegan moved down towards the end of the line, looking into the furthest man's eyes. And while sweat poured from this man's face, he showed little fear. Not even when Reegan raised the pistol to his chin.

"I'd rather not kill anyone today," Reegan nearly whispered. "But if I have to—"

"You won't."

All eyes turned to the man who spoke the words—a man three down from Reegan. Smiling, he lowered the pistol and approached his new target.

"These men served under Blake," the man said. "They're too loyal to be turned."

"And yourself?" Reegan asked.

"I'm loyal to my country," the man said. "Not to Blake. I won't die for him."

Behind Reegan, the bleeding men let out just enough of a noise beneath his gag to turn him around. Reegan could see the pleading eyes in Dustin. They shined right towards his new friend.

"Bad blood, huh?" Reegan asked of the man. "What's your name?"

"Jordan Connelly."

Reegan smiled. There would be no need to question this man's loyalty. Whatever caused a rift between Dustin, Jordan, and Blake, it was of no importance to him. He turned to the rest of the Marines. "Jordan here's just saved your lives. I'd thank him as you walk out."

The men were quickly escorted out of the room, and Reegan left with Jordan in tow before the Governor could bother to annoy him with any further discussion.

As he stepped outside towards the SUV, his assistant approached with a view screen.

"Please let it be good news," Reegan said.

"We've got a possible location for Blake," the assistant said. "Reports say we've got disturbances on road feeds towards the western edge of the province —something moving north. These are digital anomalies most likely caused by an anti-surveillance vehicle, but none are in current use in the region. We're working on getting prints sent through the Terminus to show you."

"No need. HALO must be operating it," Reegan said. "Mobilize our forces to the western Terminus. And set up a

blockade. I want every available man on this location."
Reegan turned to the silent Jordan. "Including *you.*"

"Yes sir."

Reegan climbed into his vehicle, satisfied.

This may be easier than he thought.

18

Much of the travel towards the northern district was quiet.

Out here, the world looked much like the one Blake had been used to in upstate New York—gentle rolling hills, and few cars traveling in each direction. Travel here was above ground, not below, and without the skyscrapers stretching effortlessly higher than Blake could ever imagine, it was easy to feel as if they were back in their own world.

The men they were traveling with were initially rather quiet, and sat together in the back of the vehicle, leaving Everett only the company of Roger and Blake towards the front. These men talked quietly amongst themselves but otherwise paid no attention to Blake and Roger. Clearly bored and drained from the content briefings and sleepless nights, Roger had dozed off several times in the first few hours, but Blake found himself unable to sleep. He stared patiently out the window, watching the landscape slowly alter from the broken decayed roads near HALO's hideaway, to fields of grains and fruits.

"You're looking at pretty much the only food supply," one of the men said behind Blake. He turned his head to see that one of the men had noticed his gaze, and moved forward to speak with him. "Food supply in the city is at least eighty percent synthetic. Out here, this is pretty much the only part of our province that'll grow any food."

"Reegan has control over the food supply?" Blake asked.

"Sure," the man admitted, "but there's nothing wrong with the city food. It's just bland, is all. There's nothing like the stuff that actually grows out here." He smiled slightly, and offered out a hand. "I'm Jonah."

Blake shook it. "Good to meet you. I was wondering if any of you talked."

Jonah looked back to the other men, who had similarly either dozed off, or simply weren't paying very much attention to Jonah and Blake, who sat towards the front of the vehicle. "They don't really enjoy missions like this. They think it's a waste of resources."

"So what do you think?" Blake asked.

"I think any avenue towards taking down Reegan is worth pursuing," he said. "If we can get word out there that Reegan's actually been kidnapping people this whole time and selling them off as 'duplicates,' the whole system would turn on its head."

"Were there ever clones?" Blake asked.

"Rumor has it, that was Reegan's original intent," Jonah explained. "But something was missing. Something couldn't be fixed, and he could never figure out how to clone another person. But in that research...your world was found. Why Reegan cared so much about replacing people when his empire was already formed? I have no idea. You'll have to ask him."

***

Much of the evening went by silently after this. Everett, who had been driving the vehicle, had pulled over once or twice for fresh air, but otherwise kept a constant and steady pace on the road. The cars here moved somewhat faster than Blake had been used to—cars beside them in the opposite lane sped past moving well over a hundred miles an hour, and it seemed as if speed limits weren't around this far away from the city. Because of this, what would have taken him a few days moved past in hours. By the time night had fallen, Everett mentioned that they had gone nearly two thousand miles.

In this time, HALO had sent a collection of several hundred profile shots to Blake, for him to judge via the car's view screen. Each photo contained a woman matching Blake's exhaustive description of his wife, including people within the correct age, height, hair color, eye color, and more. But with each photo Blake looked through, it became clear within seconds that it was not his wife. He reported back to Chamberlain after only twenty minutes, telling her that none matched the description.

"We'll widen our scope," she said over the comm link, "but this could take some time. For now, we've got bigger problems. You're crossing into the western sprawl of the city, and we're already seeing roadblocks."

"Keep me updated on the current route," Everett said into the receiver by the wheel. "I'll follow it as best I can. If it's a small roadblock, I should be able to talk my out of it."

"I don't understand," Roger said. He sat up in his seat and spoke clearly so that Chamberlain could hear it: "Reegan knows we're coming. Small roadblock or not, wouldn't they stop any military vehicle passing through?"

Jonah was first to speak up. "Reegan's strength is also his weakness," he said. "He can stop the major arteries of the city all he wants, but he's mobilized all available men to the area. There's hundreds of vehicles like this one, and all of them are swarming in the city. In that chaos, all we have to do is provide some proof of identification and we should be in the clear. We've had to do this more than a few times."

"Something's off," Chamberlain said. "We've studied their patterns before, and none of these roadblocks seem to be within the typical protocol of Reegan's men."

"Meaning?" Everett asked.

"Meaning, something is off," Chamberlain said. "But like I said before, we'll keep you posted."

The line cut after that, and Everett maneuvered the car through the growing traffic outside the vehicle. A two-lane road quickly widened into an eight-lane highway, and the men seated behind Roger and Blake grew antsy. Jonah in particular was spending a lot of time looking through the one-way windows, checking to see signs of a conflict.

"Relax, boys," Everett called from the driver's seat. "We're almost through the thick of it. Maybe twenty more minutes and we're on the other side of the city. From there, it's a clear shot northward."

Suddenly, the comm link roared with interference. Everett fiddled with the controls, before a clear message could come through: "Double back!"

"What?"

"You're being funneled towards a specific road north of town," Chamberlain said. Her voice was sharp and filled with worry. "There's military activity in each direction north except for this one road."

"If it's north of town," Jonah said, "we'll be fine. We can get ourselves through one roadblock. We already planned for this."

"If we're being worked into a corner, we need to turn back now," another one of the men said.

"It's now or never," Everett said. "Our only asset was the element of surprise. If we don't move through now, we're not going to be able to go through at all."

Chamberlain seemed to try to say more, but the line sputtered and decayed, and cut out completely. *Something* was interfering with their signal.

"Blake?" Roger asked. "What do you think?"

Blake's eyes turned to the anxious men, then to Everett, before returning to Roger. On one hand, moving directly into a bottleneck like this would be playing directly into Reegan's hand. On the other, without moving forward now, it would be weeks before they could get a clear shot through the city again. Reegan knew their only respite was south. He'd have more time to mobilize his force and block every road north he could find, and faster than they could outmaneuver him or slip through the fog of war. This *was* their only hope.

"I'm willing to risk it," Blake said, before looking to the men: "but only if we have an accord."

The men seemed to look to each other for guidance, but only gripped their rifles just a bit tighter. Jonah spoke for them: "Let's keep moving. Everett, how far are we?"

"Maybe a mile," he said. "Get ready."

Outside the windows, Blake could see what Chamberlain was referring to. The small high rises that had stood in small bursts to either side of the road soon ended, and the road ahead held signage that pointed north. From his perspective, he could see the city end completely several miles ahead, with one small group of men preparing a traffic stop. If it held as is, Everett and his crew would only be outnumbered by one or two.

Still, he never dropped his guard, and the men running the roadblock turned to the vehicle as it made its final approach, slowing down and rolling down its driver's side window.

"Small or not, engaging is a last resort," Everett said to the men. "Let me talk first."

The vehicle pulled to a stop and waited for the military officer outside—a bearish man obscured by a visor—to finish with the car in front of them. To either side of the road, three or four men waited lazily, rifles still on their back. Inside the car, Jonah and his men gripped the back doors of the vehicle, ready to jump out at a moment's notice. Blake waited just behind the driver's seat, his own hand wrapped around a pistol. Roger held his own gun loosely, and visibly shook with anticipation.

Finally, the officer outside approached the window. "Good evening," Blake heard him say to Everett. "Can I see some district identification?"

"Sure," Everett said. A long silence persisted afterward as Blake heard Everett pull out a card and hand it to the officer.

Something about the officer's voice was eating away at Blake. It was familiar—too familiar. Like the sound of a ghost from years past. But he couldn't quite place it.

"Sorry about this," Blake heard the officer continue. "Just a standard procedure these days. If it isn't one thing, it's another. Where are you guys heading?"

"North, near the border," Everett replied, cool as ice. "Some training exercise."

"I feel ya," the officer replied. "We got called out here for something like that." Another pause, then: "Here, you're all clear."

The voice as eating away at Blake's mind, but he couldn't place it. But something was definitely off. Even for an organization spread as thin as Reegan's, this was too easy. They would've been told to check military vehicles in the region. They would've checked to see if this vehicle was interfering with their surveillance. No, something was off.

"Oh, one more thing," the officer said. *"Does Blake know what they've done to Dustin?"*

That's when it all came rushing back.

The man's voice belonged to Jordan Connolly, Gunnery Sergeant in the Marines, and one of Blake's former squad mates. He was a man Blake hadn't seen in years—not since their time together in Afghanistan. He was loyal, devoted, and most of all, uncompromising to his own moral compass. Especially to the enemy.

And now, he stood between Blake and Casey.

Blake swung around the driver's seat, reaching around Everett and pointing his pistol directly between

Jordan's eyes. "You better have a good goddamn reason for this, Connolly."

Jordan didn't even flinch. "I didn't want to do this, Blake. But you hung Dustin out to dry. And none of the other men were brave enough to stand up for him."

"He knew more than he would ever tell me," Blake said. "He stood between me and my wife. And now, you do too."

Everett, who sat motionless between the two men, stared directly ahead to the pistol pointed out of the car, and towards the officer. "Blake—"

"*Not now.*"

"He was trying to protect you, Blake," Jordan said. "We all were. Maybe we didn't know about this place, but we knew enough. We knew that if we let you chase down Casey, you'd be killed. And you implicated him. What kind of loyalty is that?"

Blake pulled the hammer back. Fire burned in his eyes. "*Tell me why I shouldn't blow your fucking brains out.*"

"In all honesty, you probably should. You've wanted too ever since our last night in the field. Ever since I forced your hand. Either way, you're not walking away from this." Jordan backed away from the car. "Semper Fi, Blake."

No matter how much Blake wanted to, he couldn't pull the trigger. Perhaps he thought it was beneath him. Or maybe he thought it would only make things worse. But truthfully, he could almost hear Casey in that moment. Feel her telling him it wasn't right. Knowing that with each person left in his wake, he was another step further away from her.

Blake pulled the pistol back and gently released the hammer, moving back towards the back of the vehicle.

Outside of the windows, Blake could see men in riot gear emerge from several civilian vehicles. Of course, Reegan had known the whole time.

It was an ambush.

"*Move, move, move!*" Jonah cried out. The doors of the vehicle opened, and the men poured into the streets.

The streets were alive with the sound of gunfire.

19

Blake rushed outside with the other men, grabbing a rifle from the vehicle as he moved. He slammed the doors shut behind him, leaving Roger and Everett alone in the vehicle.

From what he could see, about two dozen men were descending upon them from the rear. In front of them, only six or seven stood. In their masks, Blake couldn't tell whether or not they were more of his former military friends.

At this point, he hardly even cared.

The men ducked behind the nearest vehicle, shots ringing past overhead. The rifles and weaponry here shrieked with a sound Blake hadn't heard before. Every other round seemed to be a tracer round—a shot that would leave a thin streak of color in the air, for only a second. These were designed to help aim at combatants in his world, but here? They seemed to nearly explode upon impact, shooting bursts of orange and red across the street, leaving them glowing with colored cinders.

It was a horrifying sight to behold.

"Keep them occupied!" Jonah shouted to his men. He pointed to some of his men, and to Blake. "You two! Blake! With me! We're going to clear a path forward!"

Blake's eyes turned ahead to see what could be done.

In front of them, he could see Jordan and some of Reegan's other men clearing to either side of the road. Two tall buildings had bottlenecked them inside, and if they had a chance, they could block the road entirely.

Directly in front of their own vehicle, two small sedans sped away—citizens caught in the collateral gunfire. This cleared the road for long enough, but if Blake knew anything, he knew what Jordan would be doing in this situation—using any dirty trick necessary to get his way.

Blake watched as his former squad mate ducked into the building on the left—no doubt where more firepower could be found. On the other side of the road, several more men ducked into the building on the right.

"They've got both of these buildings!" Blake shouted over the gunfire to Jonah. "We need to split up and lock both of them down before we can get out of here!"

The windshield above them shattered, sending broken glass raining down upon them. On either side of them, Jonah's men were struggling to gain ground.

Jonah turned to his two men and pointed to the building on the right: "Clear it out! We'll clear a path!"

Jonah raised up his rifle and fired several rounds behind them to the approaching force, drawing enough attention to allow the two men to run several feet, making their way inside the right building. As soon as they were clear, Jonah ducked down again and met back up with Blake.

Blake crawled low to the ground, moving to the driver's side door of their own vehicle. Bullets struck the car's metal surface and ricocheted out in several directions, littering the walls of the buildings beside them with bullet holes and keeping the air glowing with the sheen of the tracer rounds.

Once he got close enough to the driver's side door to see Everett and Roger, the door was cracked open just enough for them to talk:

"We need to leave, now!" Everett yelled. "The path ahead is clear!"

"We have to clear these buildings!" Jonah shouted behind Blake. "We don't know what kind of firepower they have!"

"If we're not back in five minutes," Blake said, "get out of here with whoever you can! Get Roger to his sister!"

Before Roger himself could protest, Everett slammed the door shut again, and Blake moved with Jonah across the street, and ducked inside the building.

As soon as the door closed behind them, Blake and Jonah stood up to examine their new surroundings. They found themselves in what appeared to be a convenience store very recently abandoned. Snacks and other trinkets were thrown about onto the floor and aisles, and apart from the lack of forced entry, it seemed to have been completely ransacked.

Ahead of them, a flight of stairs was the only way forward. The two men marched forward, ascending the stairs and into the next area of the building. Up here, the stairs turned towards a long hallway with several wooden doors dingy, green wallpaper. But as they tried to enter the hallway, a door on the left about twenty feet away opened to reveal two of Reegan's masked men, with rifles aimed right at them.

They ducked back into the stairwell as lead sliced the air above them, splintering the wooden walls and raining debris down onto them. Blake looked to the ground to see cinders of orange and red bounce downward down the stairs, before cooling off and fading away entirely.

Blake pressed his back against the wall, just inches away from the hallway. Jonah was pressed onto the opposite wall, and both held firmly to their rifles.

The shots rang out like popcorn, in short bursts of semi-automatic rounds. Blake counted quickly as to how many rounds had been fired. The men may have had the vantage point and upper hand, but they were only as powerful as the rounds they held, and based on their magazines, that wasn't nearly as many as they would have liked.

Finally, Blake heard the sound he was looking for—the small click of a magazine being lowered from a rifle.

He pivoted around the wall, firing as many rounds as he could through the wall and towards the direction of the men. He heard a distinct thud as one of the men hit the ground—a limp arm moved into view and hung outside the doorframe from his position, confirming the kill.

Blake and Jonah rushed forward, moving two more doors down and to the right before ducking inside the next room. The gunfire from Reegan's men continued less than a second after they had moved out of the line of fire, riddling the wall just a foot from Blake's position.

Jonah grabbed a magazine from his pouch and tossed to Blake, who quickly dropped his empty magazine onto the floor and reloaded.

"We're outgunned!" Jonah yelled. "We can't wait until they keep running out of ammo!" He pointed to his belt, which held only one more magazine of ammo between the two of them. "We'll run out ourselves!"

Blake nodded—he knew Jonah was right. If they continued to waste valuable ammo, they'd soon be caught in a gunfight without bullets. The only way to get to that room was finding a way to cross the remaining fifteen feet without wasting ammunition.

Blake looked around their newfound cover for ideas. They had found themselves in what looked like a small, low-income studio apartment. A kitchenette rested in one corner of the room, while the other was littered with trash and an old, metal-framed bed.

Blake ran over to the bed, lifting up the mattress to find the jackpot—the bed was held up not by several rungs of steel bars, but rather a full sheet of steel, sat on top of the frame.

"What are you doing?" Jonah shouted.

"Help me with this!" Blake called back. With some effort, the two of them were able to lift the metal sheet upwards. Standing on its end, the sheet was about three feet wide and six feet long.

"You think this will hold?" Jonah asked.

"What other choice do we have?"

Jonah nodded, and moved back towards the door. He swung his rifle out into the field of vision, and fired several rounds of suppressing fire. The enemy returned in kind, firing off about a dozen rounds from a single rifle. From the sound of it, only one man was left protecting the others.

Just as expected, another familiar click could be heard. That one man was reloading.

"Now!" Blake shouted. He lifted one end of the steel plate as Jonah ran over and lifted the other. The two maneuvered the plate out of the door and ran blindly down the hallway.

Immediately bullets struck and ricocheted off of the plate, denting the metal near Blake's face. He nearly roared under the strain of lifting the massive metal plate, closing the gap between them and the door.

Blake and Jonah threw the plate forward, knocking the last cover man down underneath it and revealing both of them to the remaining men inside—three masked men, all working around a table. As the men looked up to see that their cover fire had failed them, Blake could distinctly see an RPG grenade being prepared for firing.

One shot, and their entire vehicle could be destroyed.

Blake and Jonah took advantage of their surprise attack, and lifted their rifles to the men. They barely had a chance to react as Blake unloaded the rest of his clip, striking the men down, eliminating the threat.

But there was no time to waste.

Jonah moved forward and lifted the RPG, moving for the windows. Blake soon joined him, and both looked out onto the firefight below.

Jonah's men were losing ground badly, as several dozen of Reegan's men moved past car after car. It would be less than a minute before the enemy was on top of them.

Blake looked next to the building across the street, and was glad to see Jonah's men signaling from the window parallel to theirs—*all clear.*

"You've got one shot at this," Blake instructed Jonah. "Aim carefully."

"Blake!"

Blake turned his head to see, at the door of the room they occupied, the man they had pushed over with the steel plate was still alive. Underneath it, it was Jordan who had called his name, and crawled outwards and towards a fallen rifle.

Blake rushed forward, pushing the rifle out of reach for Jordan, and pointing his own towards his former friend. Jordan looked up, and only closed his eyes, waiting for the inevitable.

Once again, Blake found himself with the life of Jordan in his hands. And it was another several seconds for him to decide what should be done.

"Semper Fi, Jordan," Blake spat out, and turned the rifle around, striking his friend in the head with the butt of the rifle, knocking him out cold, but leaving him very much alive.

Maybe Jordan was willing to sink so low, but Blake wasn't going to.

Behind him, he could hear Jonah fire off the RPG, and a quiet silence preceded the massive explosion of shrapnel and metal that followed. He and Jonah ran from the room, back down the stairs, and met up with the rest of the men at the car. Out here, Blake could see that Roger had strategically shot a large truck nearby, engulfing the cars behind them in flames and creating a diversion long enough to get them out of there.

They piled into the back of the vehicle, and sped away into the night, leaving Jordan and the city far behind them.

They had escaped, for now.

20

After the adrenaline of the fight had subsided, Blake helped Jonah and the others tend to their wounded. Three men had been shot—two in the leg, and one in the hip. Jonah worked with the group's medic to bandage their wounds well into their journey. Soon enough, three smashed pieces of lead were lying on the metal floor, safety removed from the man.

"I would have thought you guys had evolved past bullets," Roger cautiously joked.

"Nothing's more powerful than throwing lead around," Jonah said. "At least, not yet."

Blake had taken the time to decompress—thinking about little more than the deep breaths he was taking, in and out, in and out. The entire vehicle seemed quiet enough, save for the gentle tremors that Roger emitted.

Once he seemed to gather his thoughts, Roger turned to Blake. "Who was that?"

"Jordan Connolly, one of my former men. Gunnery Sergeant. Reegan must've talked to him after we crossed over."

"He's got your old crew out against you?"

"No," Blake said. "Just him."

"Jesus," Everett murmured from the front seat.

"Report... Officer... please respond..."

The entire group turned to look to the vehicle's comm link, which had been silent ever since the firefight. So long in fact, Everett had assumed its functions had been damaged by the bullets the vehicle had taken.

"This is First Officer Everett Goodwin," Everett chimed into the microphone. "Chamberlain, is that you?"

"It's me," the voice returned. Chamberlain was being obscured by static and noise. "We've been trying to reach you for hours. What happened?"

"An ambush," Jonah said. He moved forward towards the front of the vehicle. "They found one of Blake's old military friends and set us up. We got out, but barely."

"Then you need to keep moving," Chamberlain said. "If the attack was as bad as you say, there's going to be an army on your tail."

"We made a deal," Blake spat out. "We find Roger's sister."

"You don't have time to stop in the northern districts," she said. "They'll be on you in a day. Pass straight through and head east to the Northern Base. That's an order."

With that, the line cut dead, leaving everyone with the silence of the drive once again.

"I'm sorry, Roger," Everett said. "Chamberlain has a point. And this vehicle isn't exactly invisible now. We need to get to a HALO-operated space and get to a new vehicle, or every one of Reegan's men from here to the city center will be right on top of us."

"The Northern Base is safe," Jonah chimed in. "It's our largest hub of operations for a thousand miles in any direction."

"I didn't come this far to just pass by," Roger said. The fear of the firefight seemed to fade from him. "We know where my sister is, we know where she lives."

"It's just too dangerous," Jonah said. "I'm sorry."

Blake thought for a moment. "Chamberlain said the army would be on top of us in a day. What time is it now?"

"Almost four in the morning," Everett said.

"We'll get to this northern city in a few hours, right?" Blake asked. Everett nodded, so he continued: "If this place is so small that there's no surveillance, then there's no harm in me or Roger walking around in public. We could park on the edge of town, me and Roger go inside, find Sam, and get back out by midafternoon. Chamberlain can't even contact us. She wouldn't even know we did it."

"We'd be risking everything," one of Jonah's men said. Blake turned his head to see the man, clutching to his wounded leg. "All for one person."

"If you want our cooperation," Blake said, "then we're going to find her."

Roger looked to Blake with an expressed that seemed like a mix of shock and thankfulness, but he paid it no mind.

Blake had come with Roger to the ends of their world and beyond. He wasn't about to betray his end of the deal now.

"Alright, Blake," Everett said. "We can give you six hours. But if you both don't come back after that, we're leaving."

***

So they all agreed.

Blake and Roger were given small ear monitors to report back to Everett and the rest of the group, and prepared for a long journey. As dawn arrived, the vehicle was parked on the outside of a town that appeared to be no different than Ithaca, not so long ago. The buildings were made of brick and stone, and a small town square seemed to lay in the distance.

As the two began their journey, they turned back to Everett, who reminded them: "We're going to talk to Chamberlain about our next steps, but we can only wait so long after that. Six hours. Then we leave."

"Sam's house is about two miles from here," Blake said. He had spent much of the past hour memorizing a map of the city. "We'll be back in four."

Everett nodded, and the two were on their way.

Roger hadn't spoken much since Blake had convinced the others to allow him to find Sam. Perhaps it was the indescribable pressure of seeing her again. Maybe he wondered whether or not he would even recognize her. With Roger, Blake hardly knew what he could be thinking— having come so close to death just twelve hours ago, to this.

"You alright?" Blake asked at the two moved closer and closer to town.

Roger didn't respond at first, but then suddenly nodded, as if he had delayed his own reaction. "I'm fine." After a moment, he continued. "Back at HALO...you mentioned one of your men risked lives for their own gain."

Blake was hesitant to open such old wounds, but perhaps, if it would calm Roger's nerves, he'd indulge him. "That was him," he responded. "It's the reason he's the only one of my men that's crossed over after me."

"That bad?"

Blake set out a small sigh. "It was three days before our tour ended. We had spent so much time chasing down this defector they had briefed us about. Some guy who turned and was giving everything he knew over to the enemy. We spent months and lost lives hunting this guy down. And eventually, Jordan got sick of it. He went into town, uncovered every stone, and eventually found out that this defector might be hiding away in one of the slums a few miles from our base."

Roger nodded. "And there wasn't a way to prove it?"

"No," Blake continued. "By the time we would have gotten the official okay to go in, our tour would have ended and we would've been back home. So, Jordan took matters into his own hands. He went AWOL, run into the slums in the middle of the night, and started a firefight that waged for *hours.* In the end, I sent the rest of my men in to extract him, and we ended up with four wounded men, one dead defector, and seven dead civilians."

"Jesus," Roger said. "Why'd he hate you for saving his life?"

"Because I made sure he never held a military position again."

Roger nodded, and the two stopped talking once again.

The road into town was quiet and not highly trafficked. Blake could've counted the cars that passed on a single hand as the two passed by home after home. It was surprising, even after having traveled thousands of miles already in this new world, that a 'normal' place such as this could even exist. It reminded Blake of a few half-forgotten memories of his own childhood, being free to wander the streets, knowing the neighbors and the exploring the forests nearby. The quiet solitude that was his life before his parents moved him into the big city.

That was a long time ago.

Eventually, the two came to a cobblestone road which veered into a small cluster of homes, too sparse to be called a neighborhood. Blake led the two of them down yet another turn, and soon, both approached the home at the end of the street—the home registered to a person with the same DNA of the strand of hair in Roger's notebook.

Once the two arrived at the edge of the driveway, Blake stopped walking. "I'll hang back," he said to Roger.

Roger looked over to him. "I'm—I don't...I don't know what to say."

Blake tried to smile. "You've got to do this on your own. It'll be okay."

Blake watched as Roger approached the home with hesitant steps, and knocked lightly on the white wooden door. After a long pause of silence, he knocked again. And again, nothing could be heard stirring inside the home, and no people seemed to mill about on the sidewalks and the road outside. Perhaps it shouldn't be so surprising, as it was still very early in the morning, but Blake couldn't help but feel terrible for Roger as he approached Blake with a particularly morose expression on his face.

"Let's check the town square, alright?" Blake offered. "We've still got another few hours."

Blake walked ahead of Roger and moved the two of them past the small white homes of the neighborhood and down to the city square. Here, apart from the occasional translucent view screen in the hands of those passing by, it would be easily to mistake the place for a common square in the history books. People moved from shop to shop, picking up supplies and groceries, and moved without purpose or rush.

Blake scanned the buildings and people for any signs of a person that looked similar to how Roger had described his sister, but it was of little use. Only Roger was going to be able to recognize her in this crowd.

Standing here in the center of town, Blake remembered the words Everett had shared back at HALO headquarters. Soon, once Reegan had gained enough power, places like this would be littered with cameras and his own men. Even a sleepy town like this would be overrun. It was the first time Blake had considered that this mission was about more than him or Roger. For these people, this was the difference between freedom and tyranny. Looking at things from this perspective, Blake found it hard to blame Chamberlain or Everett for wanting to move past this city entirely.

"Blake," he heard Roger say behind him.

Blake turned around to see Roger, silent and standing on uneasy feet, looking forward into one of the shops about fifty feet away. Inside, a woman about the age of Roger stood behind a counter. Her dark hair and wide eyes made it hard to mistake her for being from the same line as Roger. Still, he asked: "Is that her?"

But Roger said nothing, and Blake watched as the raven-haired woman talked pleasantly to one of the customers in her shop. From the back of the store, a tall man approached her, and the two kissed, before the man moved back behind the counter. She turned back to the customers and gave them a wave as they moved away, collecting their groceries and exiting the store. As she did, her eyes looked to Blake and Roger, and her smile faded. *Did she recognize him?*

Blake turned to Roger, but he was already looking away, moving back out of town. Blake jogged a few paces to catch up. "Roger!" He called out, closing the gap between them. "Now what?"

Roger looked to Blake, and smiled for the first time that day. "Let's go get your wife."

21

Blake and Roger returned to the vehicle immediately afterwards, and Jonah, Everett, and the rest of the men seemed glad to be leaving the town behind. And judging by the silence that stood between them, the men seemed smart enough not to bother Roger by asking what had ultimately happened between him and his sister.

Outside of the car, the cities and towns faded back into obscurity, and the vehicle weaved its way through mountains and valleys. This far north, Everett explained to Blake, a massive mountain range lined the border between this province and the next. It was the only natural barrier stopping Reegan from expanding completely. And soon, even it wouldn't be enough. Economically speaking, Everett explained, Reegan was close enough to buying control of the other provinces. From there, the ends were limitless.

The sleepless night the group had suffered meant that much of this journey was spent in silence, as most of the men slept. All except for a few—Roger, who scribbled away endlessly in his journal, Everett, who was driving, Jonah, and Blake.

"Hey, Blake," Jonah asked at one point during the trip. Blake blinked away the exhaustion he was feeling and turned around to him. "About last night—"

"You're wondering why I let Jordan live," Blake said, finishing his thought for him.

"You had the chance to kill him," Jonah said. "Twice, even. Lord knows he deserved it."

"It's complicated," Blake said. "Me and him, Dustin, all the other guys...we had each other's back in parts of our world that are no different than hell itself. Even after a betrayal like that...I don't know. I wasn't going to do it. Even if I should have. That's blood I don't want on my hands. I've got enough to keep me up at night as it is."

Jonah seemed to understand in a way only military men could—a cold face that's seen far too much for his own good.

***

The vehicle weaved its way off of the main road and onto a gravel pathway, just inches away from the sheer cliffside. To make matters worse, the sky opened up as they traveled, and thick sheets of rain came down hard upon the road, creating a messy path of rocks and mud to traverse. Blake couldn't help but feel a tinge of fear in situations like these. Firefights like the one just a day ago weren't as terrifying, simply because of Blake's ability to control his own actions. Here, he was at the mercy of Everett's driving and the road. One chance accident could send them tumbling downward, cutting their mission short here.

It was a high price to pay for the privacy of HALO's northern base, but once the gravel cleared out and the vehicle moved to flatter ground, Blake could understand why.

The group came upon a building that looked about half the size of HALO's main base of operations, although Blake knew better than to assume there weren't many underground tunnels throughout this region. As they approached, Everett explained:

"This was another one of Reegan's failed hideaways," he said. "Or rather, his father's. Any more north and the land becomes completely uninhabitable for a hundred miles."

"It seems like he's abandoning more buildings than he should," Blake noted. "I don't understand why he hasn't sent men out this far."

"It's all a farce with him," Jonah said, now fully awake. "He's been expanding too fast for his own good. Without good evidence, he can't justify the cost of checking areas of the province like this. Not yet."

"How well do you know these men?" Roger asked.

"Enough to know they won't be too pleased to see us," Jonah replied.

The vehicle sputtered to a stop, and the doors opened, leading Everett, Jonah, and the rest of the men out into the rain. Blake helped one of the wounded men out of the vehicle, and the group rushed to get out of the wet, cold open air. The steel doors to the compound opened with a low buzz before they had closed the gap between them, and the group entered without incident.

HALO men waited inside for them, and silently collected their three wounded, taking them no doubt towards a medical bay. Soon after, a tall man with sharp, brown eyes approached, and identified himself to the group as the head of the HALO compound.

He spoke very little, and didn't bother to greet Blake or Roger. Instead, he motioned for the remaining men to enter a separate room, leaving Everett, Jonah, Blake, and Roger alone by the entrance doors.

Everett moved next, leading the remaining group down a series of dull, grey hallways. The single lights that lined these halls were spread so few and far between, half of the journey could hardly be seen.

"They're not a talkative bunch, as you could see," Everett explained. "They don't like the fact that they have to give up one of their own anti-surveillance vehicles for us, but Chamberlain ordered it. If we keep driving that bullet-riddled thing outside, we'll be tracked for sure."

"So where to now?" Roger asked.

JASON YORMARK

"The conference room."

As he said the words, Everett stopped at one of the many doors that lined the hallway, and pushed it open. Inside, a room similar to the one back at HALO's headquarters could be seen—a table sat in the center of the room, adorned by a single light above.

The four men took their seats around the table, and Everett moved to the comm link on the center of the table, pressing several buttons before the link activated with a hiss.

"Any luck pinpointing Reegan's bases after last night?" Everett asked.

Chamberlain sighed. "We already knew about his stronghold in the west. We couldn't find anything else. A small number of his force moved north after that fight, but your guess is as good as ours as to where they could be. Without the surveillance footage, both us and Reegan are blind."

"A blessing and a curse," Jonah mused.

"You'll stay the night there," Chamberlain continued, "but you need to keep moving. There's a few places in the northern suburbs we think Reegan might be based in. There's an inordinate amount of military activity there. We think he might be hiding something."

"Any more photos I can look through?" Blake asked.

"We're assembling another thousand for tonight. There'll be a tablet in your room for you to scout it out. Anything else?"

A moment of silence.

"Good," Chamberlain said. "We'll be in touch."

The line went dead soon after.

***

The rest of the evening moved in a blur for Blake. From that room, he had been led to a cafeteria, where he ate food as cold and as wet as the weather outside. Afterwards, he stayed quietly in his and Roger's given room—another

148

small concession, made up of just two bunk beds and a table in the corner. After a shower, Blake sat at the table, flipping through the endless photos of women that Chamberlain had sent his way.

Roger, however, was nowhere to be found. After what had happened with his sister, the man hadn't spoken privately to Blake in any capacity, and once dinner was over, he had requested to access the archives at their disposal. Maybe he was burying his head in self-made work, or just distracting himself. Blake couldn't be sure.

Finally, Roger entered the room sometime after eleven, when most of the rest of the base had gone to bed. Blake worked under the light of a single lamp, and hardly looked up at his friend's entrance.

"Anything?" Blake heard Roger ask from behind him.

Blake didn't respond, and wondered if he had given Chamberlain the right specifications for Casey. Each girl in the photo hardly looked like the woman he loved. After another few photos, he set the tablet down for a minute and turned his chair to Roger, who was undressing for bed.

"You're okay, right?" Blake asked. He felt uncomfortable trying to reach out to Roger, but felt like he had no other choice. "This morning wasn't—"

"I'm good, thank you." Roger said. His genuine tone seemed to show he wasn't just saying it, either. "I've got my answers. Now we just need to get you yours."

"I don't know how much longer I can deal with these endless photos," Blake said, rejecting another four photos on screen. "None of these are even close to Casey. There's got to be a better way to do this."

"Maybe there isn't," Roger admitted. "I've looked in the archives and asked Everett more questions than I should. In many ways, this world is far beyond our own, but in cases like this—there's not much else that can be done."

Blake nodded, and stood up from the table, needing a break from all of the photos. To clear his mind, he took a long shower in the communal restroom, and returned to see Roger had already fallen asleep. Blake thought for a moment about trying his own hand at resting—there was a long day tomorrow and they had been told to be ready by six.

However, Blake resigned himself to the table once again, and flipped through the endless photos. Maybe if he just finished off this group of a thousand, he thought to himself. Then, he could check off another thousand on the ride out of here tomorrow.

"Hey," a voice said at the door. Blake turned his head to see Jonah standing in the open doorframe. "You should really get some sleep."

"So should you."

Jonah cleared his throat. "I never got around to thanking you," he said. "That stunt you pulled with the bed saved our asses. I wouldn't have thought of that."

"You don't need to thank me," Blake said. "We did what we had to do."

"Always," he responded. "If you don't mind me asking...how did you meet your wife?"

Blake smiled. "Doing what I've always done. We were deployed out in some of the worst parts of our world, and I took a bullet during a raid like last night. Nothing serious—just grazed me. But the woman that patched me up afterwards wasn't like the other nurses. She didn't thank me for my service, or just treated me like another patient...she just sort of understood. Here we were, wanting to kill men that wanted to kill us, and she helped us without caring too much about the politics of it all or who she was helping. She just wanted to help. She made me a better person. Without her...I'm just back to where I used to be."

"Stick with it, Blake," Jonah said. "You'll find her. After coming this far, what's a couple thousand photos?" Jonah moved from the doorframe and began to close the door. "Goodnight, Blake."

"Good night."

Blake took another minute away from the tablet, lost in thought. Having to look through photos like this was draining enough. Talking about Casey like that was even worse. He could only hope Roger was right about him finding his answers.

So he continued flipping through photo after photo after photo. Eleven at night soon turned to three in the morning, and Blake found himself lying in bed, struggling to keep his eyes open, looking through photo after photo. He tried to blink the sleep away, but it was no use.

Just a few more, he thought to himself.

He moved past five more photos.

Just a few more.

Another three.

Another two.

Four more.

Another eight.

And then—

Blake's heart stopped as the next photo appeared on the screen. It was a blurry photo, from a surveillance camera rather far from the citizens on the street. The woman in the center of the photo was a woman far older than Casey, and was no doubt the reason the photo had been sent to him. This woman looked cold and miserable in the rains that had fallen during the taking of this photograph.

But, three rows behind her, moving just near the edge of the frame, was a slender blond woman. Even through the blurriness, Blake could see her slender frame, deep-seated eyes, and soft jaw. But it wasn't just the way she looked—it was the way she carried herself. It was her confidence in the rain. It was an instant moment of memory:

Blake and Casey had been separated for some time after the night that wounded him, and after the night the two had truly met. The wound he suffered and told Jonah about happened on the same night Jordan had chosen to betray their cause and go AWOL. Instead of being routed home the next day, Blake had spent another two months in military trials, explaining the events of the evening, and condemning Jordan to dishonor and virtual banishment from the armed forces.

It was a long and slow process, and the contact he was able to hold with Casey was minimal at best. But still, their desire persisted. Blake would write notes to her when he could after she had returned home. She wrote about the winter snows that had fallen in the city, as Blake remained in the desolation of the desert. She sent her love long before she would ever say the words.

Finally, the time came for Blake to return home. He walked alone with a single bag and civilian clothes through the crowded halls of John F. Kennedy International Airport. After his ordeal, there wasn't another day he wanted to spend in his old uniform.

He watched from a distance as the other men ran into the loving arms of their wives, their sisters, and their daughters. Families reunited with husbands, and children to their mothers—the pleasant conclusion of war.

He walked alone to baggage claim and pulled out what little he carried with him across the pond. Then, he moved outside and waited for a taxi, under the awning in the frigid winter rain. He thought of little else but the paperwork left to file until he had made his time a thing of the past. That, and the visit he would be paying to Casey sometime soon.

Except, he didn't need to wait a moment longer. Casey wrapped her arms around him from behind as he hailed for a taxi, nearly giving him a stroke. It was another moment of shock before he realized that Casey had personally searched for his flight and made the effort to drive all this way.

She was soaking wet when she hugged him. She quickly explained that she had parked in the wrong terminal and had to run a quarter mile in the rain to surprise him. And when Blake tried explain how sorry he had felt, she reminded him not to be too sorry—that they would soon have to run the quarter mile back, but this time, together.

She had done it all for him.

And he realized right then, she was perfect.

Blake pushed himself out of bed, as awake as ever. And for the first time since he lost Casey, Blake eyes began to water, and he found himself weeping. But even still, he could not take his eyes off of that photo, and Casey's familiar form, waiting for him in the rain. He couldn't look away.

He had found her.

He had *finally* found her.

22

Jordan's patience was wearing thin.

After the abysmal failure just a night ago, Reegan's men had unceremoniously picked him up and shipped him off to yet another location he didn't know or understand.

Ever since being taken to this world, the communication between Jordan, Reegan's men, and Reegan himself had been indirect at best. There had been no briefings, no time to cope with the reality of the situation or even the culture and ethics of the brave new world he found himself in. Even after his failure, when Jordan was expecting a full reprimand from the elusive and threatening Reegan, there hadn't been so much as a message sent between them.

Now, he waited in yet another room—this one filled to the brim with paintings and objects he could seldom recognize. Outside of these four falls, Jordan could hear the familiar pattern of a waltz—no doubt he had been taken to a back room of some gala or ball.

But the question remained: *why?*

Jordan sat separately from his assigned bodyguards, nursing the growing knot on his head from where Blake had struck him. The wound had served a physical purpose, surely, but the shock of the reaction from Blake was what had struck Jordan. In all his years, Jordan had never known Blake to be a man of mercy. Hell, Lord knows he wasn't either. Maybe it had been Casey that softened him up after the wars, but the very idea that the Blake Collier would allow him to live was weighing on him.

Luckily, he didn't have to dwell for too much longer, as the door opened and Reegan's familiar assistant entered the room—this time, in black tie. The gentleman's receding hairline wasn't serviced by the slicked back look this man had chosen. He reeked of nepotism, or at least his gross incompetence seemed to suggest that. If anything, this particular unnamed man was simply an extra set of eyes and ears to Reegan.

"Jon would like to see you now," the assistant said, looking everywhere but Jordan's eyes. Following the order, Jordan rose and followed the meek assistant out into a main hallway, decorated in similar fashion to the room he had been in before. About every twenty feet or so, Jordan passed couples dressed similarly to the assistant, each giving him a lingering stare before returning their attention to the artwork that lined the walls. Even Jordan felt uncomfortable at the sight, feeling particularly out of place in his tattered tactical wardrobe. Perhaps if Reegan had provided his assets with the proper attire, he wouldn't be so distracting to his guests.

Finally, the two arrived at yet another room off to the side and around a corner, where Jordan nodded to the two bodyguards that stood watch. As he crossed the threshold of the door, he could now see Reegan, seated with several other guests, smiling and laughing. Here, the assistant lifted an arm to Jordan's torso to stop him.

"I'll get you a refreshment," the man said, turning to a wet bar at the side of the room. Jordan was grateful for the sentiment, at least—if he was going to have to continue to endure this gaudy party, he had better at least be drunk.

"Jordan!" Reegan called out from the table. Jordan turned his head to see that Jon had noticed his arrival. Reegan stood and excused himself from his party guests, before approaching Jordan with an uncomfortable smile and a tight handshake. "Glad to see you've made it out in one piece!"

"I didn't want to interrupt," Jordan said, low. Reegan's assistant returned to his side, and handed him a glass of amber liquid, before leaving without another word. After a sip, Jordan recognized it to be some sort of cider.

"Please, trust me," Reegan said. "It's much better this way. You're sparing me from an awful lot of dismal conversation. Please," he motioned to the door.

Jordan followed Reegan back out, into the hallway, and the two walked slowly as they talked:

"I was pleased to hear you suffered no real losses," Reegan said, "well, other than a few of my own men."

"I take full responsibility for the failure of the mission," Jordan said. He felt it best to apologize now, rather than risk disrespecting a man as powerful as this. "Had I known Blake's continued capabilities I wouldn't have directed your men the way I did."

"Oh, I understand what happened," Reegan said. "I might not know war strategy, but I know how to secure a different kind of empire. Your hubris is what ensured the mission's collapse. You had anticipated all options, except for failure. Which is *precisely* why Blake got away from you."

Jordan knew better than to respond to such a statement. Instead, he nodded, sipped his drink, and let Reegan continue:

"I've done it before, you know. Thought I had secured enough votes, or backed the right horse. Don't feel too bad about it. HALO thinks they can hide up north, but they're not stupid. They lack the most important tool of all—time. I'm in no rush to take them down; I've got all the time in the world. The longer they wait, further they dig their own grave."

"So, we wait?" Jordan finally asked.

"As long as necessary," Reegan said. "You'll be well-provisioned with my men, armed and ready, so don't worry about your time spent idling about. Although I need to warn you—"

"Jon?" Came a woman's voice from behind them, interrupting Reegan. The two of them turned around to face a middle-aged brunette woman, dressed elegantly in a striking grey dress. Reegan smiled. "You promised me this would be a night off."

"And it is," Reegan said. Jordan watched as Reegan leaned in to kiss the woman. Afterward, Reegan turned back to Jordan. "My wife, Anne."

"A pleasure," Jordan said, shaking the woman's hand. Before he could further introduce himself, Reegan turned back to her.

"It will be just a moment. We're nearly done," he said. She nodded, and left as soon as she had arrived. He turned back to Jordan. "I keep Anne comfortably distant from affairs such as this. Keeps her happy, which keeps me happy."

"As you were saying?" Jordan reminded Reegan.

"Oh, right!" Reegan said. "What I was saying, was that I like you, Jordan. I want to continue to work with you. I believe in second chances, and so I'm willing for completely forget that foolish little mistake you made that got the men I gave to you killed. There's going to be no punishment for it. I would just like to gently remind you, however, that the next time Blake and HALO rear their heads, it may be wise rethink your strategy. I hope you take this opportunity seriously, because *there will not be another.*"

"Understood," Jordan said. He finished his drink, and Reegan took the empty glass from him soon after.

"Now, if you'll excuse me," Reegan said, "I'll be returning to my wife now."

And with that, Jon Reegan left Jordan alone in the hall. And if there was one thing Jordan had learned from this specific interaction with Reegan, it was that he was far from joking. He would not receive the same mercy from Reegan as he had from Blake. And, if he failed to capture Blake, he may still cost Jordan his life yet.

So where the hell was he?

23

The following day moved past in little more than a blur.

Blake was able to pass the photo of Casey off to HALO's headquarters, and they had a correct match within just a few hours. As luck would have it, their previous trajectory only needed to be slightly altered, as Casey's location was somewhere in the sprawling suburbia of one of the northeastern districts—the same area that HALO was tracking for Reegan's operations. They were close to killing two birds with one stone—the discovery and recovery of Blake's wife, as well as the discovery of Reegan's centralized base for his human trafficking operation. If such a location was to be discovered, HALO could focus all of its efforts onto dismantling Reegan's empire with the truth about what was done.

And Blake would have his wife again.

The traveling party loaded up into a new anti-surveillance vehicle and traveled for the rest of that day, and into the rest of that night. Outside, the jagged peaks devolved into rolling hills, and the crew found themselves within a deep rainforest. Thick sheets of rain pelted the car as it weaved its way out of the barren landscape of the north to the civilization of the east, but it was not an easy drive—nor a quick one. Everett had been beaten down by the relentless drive, and soon taught Roger how to operate the vehicle. He and Jonah switched out with Everett to keep the vehicle moving at a fast pace as to not be discovered, leaving Blake ample time to think on the experience he was soon to have.

"She has a life here, Blake," Chamberlain had said to him over the comm link once most of the others had fallen asleep. "When she was moved here, she was forced to forget her old life. We don't know how Reegan does it. We don't know if we'll be able to recover those memories."

"I know," Blake said. Still, the knowledge was no more or less comforting than any of the other misfortunes they had uncovered along the way.

"We can get you as far as where she is, but once you're inside that home, we have no control over what truth you find out about her," Chamberlain continued. "She lives in a townhouse just minutes away from where we've seen heavy military activity. You may only have minutes to decide what needs to be done."

"I'll do what I have to," Blake said. "I always have."

After that conversation had ended, Blake tried to get some sleep, but found himself staring upwards into the ceiling of the vehicle. The gentle vibrations and rocking of the car was enough to send him into a half sleep-like state. Enough to keep his mind on thoughts of Casey, but not enough to obtain any rest. The exhaustion and sleep deprivation of the past several nights was beginning to wear on his body, and Roger had already voiced his concerns to him before. Counting the hours, Blake was fairly confident he had gotten no real sleep in well over three days.

It reminded him greatly of a similar car ride from his past.

Blake's parents had removed him suddenly from the small town he was from. And while he was so young at the time he could only remember blurred faces and half-remembered buildings from his former home, the journey away, he remembered.

His parent woke him in the middle of the night to take him into the city. He moved with them as they sped through the night. He could still remember their shouting voices as he was flung about in the back of the car with the lesser things. He never really got to find out what had caused their hurry. Now that he was older, he certainly would have asked if he had been given the chance.

It was three years past before he was picked up by scary men in black from his school. His parents, as it turned out, had been caught in the crossfire of two rival gangs, in the heat of the violence of the inner city. Wrong place, wrong time. He didn't rest well after that moment. Never ever, not truly.

And there would be no rest until he found his wife—a moment years in the making, that seemed only a few short hours away now.

"Blake?" he heard a voice ask him. Blake sat up in his chair to see Roger, looking at him with wide open eyes.

"You should sleep, Roger," Blake said. "Whatever it is, we can talk about it then."

"No, it's just—" Roger stammered out. He moved a hand to his head at scratched at his hair. "Look, this whole thing's been a damn nightmare, but thank you. For everything."

Blake looked down for a moment, before reconnecting: "There's nothing to thank, Roger. We're here because of you as much as we are because of me."

"We didn't have to see Sam," Roger said. "You didn't have to push them to take me to her and you did. I won't forget that."

Blake cracked a smile. "I know you'd do the same for me."

Roger seemed to get to the crux of his conversation— his face slowly lowering with his gaze. He said in quiet voice: "I hope she's how you remember."

Blake thought for a moment, then:

"Me too."

***

Morning came slow—the gentle orange rays of the first light of day hovered over the horizon and shone into the car from the front windows, awakening Jonah and the rest of the men. Everett pulled over soon after and traded the wheel for Roger's seat—taking a nap as Roger followed the GPS and moved them towards town.

"You're about two hours away," Chamberlain explained. "As far as we can tell, she's still at home."

"We'll be in and out of there as fast as we can," Jonah said. "Who knows, it might even be a good thing if we take our time."

"There's no need for unnecessary risk," Chamberlain said. "We're getting more and more evidence that there's a considerable base of operations for Reegan there. And he won't hesitate to mobilize everyone he has for us. He's shown it before. In fact, I'm heading that way myself. If something goes down, it may be all or nothing."

"Let's hope it doesn't come to that," Roger said, growing more comfortable, surrounded by his militant peers. "You guys have any more specificity than a region for this base?"

"We've got our eye on a couple of large textile mills north of the city you're currently in," Chamberlain said. "They're low security, but there's no surveillance out there, either. If it's one of those, a fully-armed HALO strike force could bring it down...but we would have to know we're right before making that sort of call."

Chamberlain signed off soon after, leaving the anticipation of their arrival entirely within Blake's mind. The last two hours of the trip sailed by quickly, and soon enough, the vehicle sputtered to a stop outside of a quaint townhouse. Blake had been so consumed in his own mind, he hadn't realized they were so close.

"Do you want someone to come with you?" Jonah asked Blake. He took several seconds to respond.

"No," Blake said. "I'll go alone."

"You have five minutes," Everett said, wiping the sleep from his eyes. "Take long enough, and we'll have to go in ourselves."

"I understand," Blake said. He moved past Jonah and the other men, and cracked open the back doors.

Outside, the light came shining through the cracked door, blinding Blake momentarily. Once his eyes re-adjusted, he found himself standing just on the edge of a small road. Town homes lined this street like the suburbs of San Francisco back home—all moving down a clear hill, towards a city in a valley.

Blake took careful steps onto the driveway of what was Casey's current home—a home painted bright blue, clean and elegant amongst the rest of its peers. A home so similar to the one Blake had once planned for them to retire to. The kind of home that could convince even him to leave the streets of New York.

He approached, climbing the five wooden steps onto the front porch of the home. He moved his hand to the door, and knocked three times.

After an agonizing half-minute, the door didn't open. Inside, no person stirred.

Blake's eyes turned back to the vehicle, where he could see—even through the tinted windows—the faces of his friends. Those who had sacrificed so much and gone so far to see a moment that appeared not to come.

But Blake wasn't going to let anything stop him at this point. No time limit, no travel companions, not Reegan…nothing.

He took a step back, lifted his boot, and kicked the door in.

The door gave way with a sickening crunch, swinging fully open, slamming into a wall, and nearly shutting again before Blake pushed his way inside.

In here, the house was just as perfect as the outside. Almost too-perfect; with wooden floors stretching from here to the staircase, to the displayed china on the far left wall.

Blake continued inside, moving to the right and into what appeared to be a living room. In here, two couches faced the wall, which held a fireplace. A large translucent screen was mounted near what appeared to be a kitchen. The room smelled of fresh linens and early morning.

And her.

Blake moved further inside, approaching the framed photos that stood on top of the fireplace. Several photos of a man Blake didn't know, in places he had never seen.

And then there was the center photo—a wedding photo. In it, the man swung his bride from him in the middle of a wedding dance. They were surrounded by countless other strangers, all beaming with the joy of a nascent relationship forming right in front of them.

The bride herself smiled brighter than Blake had ever seen—except, of course, on her own wedding day with himself.

They had married in a field, with close friends and family being the only attendees. They had chosen a traditional ceremony. And the moment Blake lifted the veil from her face, the way she smiled at him through loose strands of her blond hair, was an image he had never forgotten. No war, no violence, and no time could ever remove that smile.

And it was the same smile she showed to the stranger holding her in this photo, on another wedding of hers, a world away.

"Who the hell are you?"

Blake turned around to see a disheveled woman standing in the doorframe between the front entrance and the living room. Her left hand gripped tightly on what looked to be a kitchen knife. She was dressed in little more than a morning robe, and looked to Blake with sharp, cold eyes.

It was Casey.

24

"Casey," Blake said aloud. His heart was pounding so loud in his chest, he was worried she could hear it even ten feet away from him. Aside from her name, he knew little else to say.

The two of them were locked in a fearful stance; Casey's eyes narrowed towards him, showing a fear and an anger he had never seen her show him. She positioned herself in a defensive position, holding the tip of the blade slightly downwards and out, toward him.

"Who are you?" Casey sputtered out in a hurry. "What are you doing here?"

Blake looked down for a moment, only to see that in the rush, he was still holding Casey's wedding photo with another man. In this moment, every second felt like a cruel nightmare, every action felt wrong. In all his years, he had never experienced anything even close to the feelings surging through him at the moment.

"You don't remember?" he asked her. He couldn't hide the vulnerability in his eyes as he spoke. "I'm your husband."

"What are you talking about?" Casey asked back. "I think you're confused."

Blake tried to think of the next thing to say, but found himself looking back at the photograph, looking longingly into the eyes of his wife.

"I can get you help," Casey said, her voice sounding less antagonistic now. "I can call someone. Maybe we could find your wife."

Hot tears burned on Blake's face. "You are my wife."

"I'm sorry," she said back. "I'm afraid you're mistaken."

"You just don't know it," Blake said. He took two steps towards her, only to watch her take two steps back, keeping a safe enough distance. "My name is Blake Collier. We met on a tour in Afghanistan. You..you surprised me in the rain when I came back. You came all that way...before you were taken from me."

"I don't know what to say, Blake," she said, saying his name with a cold and quiet tone. "I don't know the places you're talking about. I've been here my whole life. Now, I know we can get you some help, you just need to...to calm down, alright? I can get the phone. I can call for help."

Before Blake could respond, the distant sound of a door opening sent low vibrations through the home. Blake's eyes bolted to the sound of the noise—which seemed to come from the back of the house.

"Honey, stay there a second!" Casey called out to the voice. They both heard the door close behind the new arrival.

"You're up?" the voice said back. Footsteps approached, coming closer and closer. "I thought you said you were sleeping in—"

"You need to wait there," Casey interrupted. "Just—just stay in the kitchen, alright?"

But he didn't listen. Instead, Blake watched as a man approached the living room from the kitchen, newspaper in hand. He wore only a white undershirt and boxers.

"What are you talking about—" he managed to say, before seeing Blake and Casey, frozen in the living room. He too, stopped in place, several feet away. "What's going on?"

This was the man in the photograph.

Casey's new husband.

***

Outside, Roger had counted every second that passed since Blake went inside. It had been almost seven minutes since he had left the vehicle, and each person that could see out of the window was desperate to see what was happening. But all they could see was the broken door, and nothing further.

"Roger," Jonah said, cutting the tension, "we need to leave."

"*He needs more time*," Roger almost shouted back. "How would you react if you saw your wife for the first time in years? We need to help him."

"Her husband could be in there," Everett said. "There's too many variables at stake for us to help him."

"Husband?" Roger asked. "She's re-married?"

"She's filling in for a person that died on this side of the bridge," Jonah explained. "Her alternative here had a whole life that she's taken the place of. She doesn't remember who he is."

"Blake should have known that," Roger said. "You should have told him!"

"He knew," Everett said. His tone was quiet and firm. "He saw her dossier. He knew what he was walking into. I just don't think he ever wanted to admit it. Clearly not to you."

Over them, the comm link sputtered on, jolting every man in the vehicle. "You need to move. *Now*," Chamberlain said to them. "Reegan's men are already on their way."

"Blake's still inside," Everett said. "He needs another minute—"

"You don't have another minute!" Chamberlain shouted back at him. "We underestimated his forces here. You've got half an army moving towards you. If you don't leave in the next ten seconds, they'll track you to the rendezvous point. This is a direct order."

"We can't leave him! He's the reason half of you are still alive," Roger practically begged. "He's the reason I'm alive."

Above them, a distinct rumble began to be audible— even Roger knew it to be the sound of a helicopter. And more than one at that.

"I'm sorry," Everett said. "I really am."

Before Roger could respond, he felt Jonah's hands behind him, grabbing both of his arms, immobilizing him. He immediately began to squirm, fighting to be free, but it was of little use. Outside, the world started moving again, and Everett began to speed away from the home, and away from Blake. "Stop, goddamn it!" He shouted at them. "Stop! You told him you'd go in after him! You can't leave!"

But the vehicle never stopped moving.

***

"Blake, this is my husband, Robert," Casey said, introducing the two, who looked to each other with more and more confusion and anger. "Robert, this is Blake. He's a little confused and he needs some help."

"I don't need help," Blake said. "Casey, please—"

"Casey?" she asked. The way she said her own name seemed foreign to her lips. "I don't know who that is."

Blake loosened his grip on the photograph, sending it clattering onto the hardwood floor below. He took several steps towards Casey, and this time, she didn't step back. Instead, she lowered the knife she held and looked him straight in the eye.

"Your name is Casey Collier," Blake said, "and you are my wife."

"You need to back up," came harsher words from Robert, who began to approach. "I don't know what your problem is, but you need to leave. Now."

Blake looked up to see Robert trying to close the distance between them. Maybe his mind hadn't allowed him to consider the true reality of the situation, or perhaps he just didn't want to accept it, but Blake suddenly felt a burning rage for this man.

It was as Chamberlain said; he thought of Casey as a duplicate of whatever happened to his wife, but in reality? It was his money—his decision that stole her from him. He was responsible for the past two years of hell Blake had gone through. And that fact rushed to his head so fast and so painfully, Blake immediately stepped forward and landed a punch straight into the man's face.

He fell down in a heap, and Casey let out a loud scream.

But it wouldn't stop Blake. Not now. He jumped on top of Robert while he lay prone on the ground, pinning his arms and legs with his own. He straddled Robert and swung a wild fist into his right cheek, sending spit and blood flying to his left. Blake swung his left hand next, and began to unleash a flurry of punches onto the poor man's face.

Robert writhed underneath Blake, but he would be no match for a Marine such as this. Instead, he wiggled an arm free and held it up to his face, trying to protect himself from Blake's onslaught.

And that was when a sharp pain shot through Blake's shoulder.

He craned his head up, momentarily shocked at the pain. He looked up just fast enough to see Casey's foot strike him in the face, sending him reeling back, off of Robert and onto the hard wood. From his vantage point, he could see Casey grabbing at Robert's face, checking to see if he was okay.

Blake reached back and found that the hilt of Casey's kitchen knife was embedded into his left shoulder. She had stabbed him in the back with the knife, and used that moment to kick him off of her husband. The blade had only sunk an inch or two into Blake's flesh, but the pain of who had done it hurt far more.

Blake pulled the knife out of his back with a thick grunt, and stood up, fully prepared to re-engage the man that had stolen his wife.

But he never got the chance.

The sounds of shattering glass ripped through the house, shocking them all. Blake looked to his left to see that the living room window had been smashed in, and scores of men in black were pouring into the home.

Reegan had found them.

Blake stood up with the knife, charging at the first man rushing towards him. He tried to stab through the man's vest, but it was no use.

The man grabbed Blake's face, and smashed it down into the glass table, rendering him inert.

From this sideways position, he could see the men surrounding Casey and Robert, forcing them to the ground and handcuffing them, before thick black bags were forced over their heads.

"Casey!" Blake shouted. He could feel the heel of another man on the small of his back, pinning him to the floor. "Casey!" He shouted again.

His head was lifted high enough from the floor for another man to slip a bag over his own head, and he saw nothing but blackness.

25

Roger had to be restrained the entire journey from the home of Blake's wife to the rendezvous point. It was only after the vehicle had pulled into the location—an abandoned textile mill east of town—that they would let him go. Roger pulled his hands out from Jonah's grip, rubbing at his wrists, before turning to Everett.

"What have you done?" He asked.

"What I had to," Everett replied, equally as cold.

The ground unloaded the vehicle and rushed inside, to find several other HALO men. There must had been twenty to forty in total, all biding their time in the empty, decaying room.

Once they had arrived, the comm link was re-activated, and Chamberlain came back on the line.

"We're about three hours out," she said. "We're traveling as fast as we can without getting spotted. What happened back there?"

"We don't know," Everett said. "We had to leave. Reegan must have prepared for us to intercept Casey. They must have known where Casey had been this entire time."

"What kind of organization leaves a man behind like that?" Roger shot at the microphone, gathering the attention of the other men who didn't know him. "We could've have saved Blake in under a minute, and you left him behind like collateral damage."

"There's nothing we could do, Roger," Chamberlain said. "And we're just as disappointed as you are. Without Blake, Reegan has a huge upper hand here. And with all the activity in the area, as soon as me and my men arrive, we're going to have to leave. We don't know how much Reegan knows about us. The wrong move here, and there won't *be* a HALO after today."

The line cut dead after that, and the men began to disperse to sit, and to wait.

"What do you think they're doing to him?" Roger asked Jonah. But Jonah only sighed, and turned his head.

"God only knows."

***

Blake felt himself move in and out of consciousness as he was transported. He felt his head smash against walls and floors—and he was forced to walk several feet before being thrown back down and dragged. The wound on his back bled so much and so often, he could feel the wetness of his back sticking to his shirt.

He was dragged across dirt and grass, then concrete and polished steel. It was the same sort of nightmarish scenario uncovered in the darkest parts of war. The sensory deprivation confused Blake to the point where he wasn't sure if it had been several hours or several days since he had been captured, and yet all he could think about was the sight of his wife, being bound and bagged like some common animal. Like himself.

Finally, he felt the cold bite of steel on his back as he was presumably lifted onto a table. He felt his hands and legs being pulled to their absolute limits, then shackled down with more steel. From there, the footsteps dissipated, and Blake could only guess that he was now alone.

Until the bag was ripped from his head, and a blinding light was shone into his eyes.

"It's been a long time coming for me to see you," a voice croaked from above Blake. "Longer than you know."

Blake's vision began to focus in waves, and soon enough, he could make out the form of a tall, dark man looming over him. He began to look around the room for other clues of his whereabouts, but all he could see was the darkness around him and the blinding light above. "Reegan," he said through clenched teeth.

"Jon in fine; well, in fact, anything is fine. By the end of the night, you won't have the slightest idea of where you are, who you were, or whatever this whole mess was about. And then I'll return to running my province —something I was *very* good at until you came along."

"You're a wanted man, Reegan," Blake said. "You've got enemies around every corner. HALO's going to—"

"HALO?" Reegan asked aloud, repeating after Blake. "Christ, Blake, I thought you were smart enough to know I'm unconcerned about a group as small as *HALO*. But since you're so interested…" Reegan bent down below Blake's field of vision, and soon produced a view screen. He moved to show a photo on it to Blake—photos of a decaying building, in some unknown location. "We've easily tracked down HALO, thanks to you. In fact, we've got enough intel to know their leader will be arriving shortly. We'll let them have their last night together. Tomorrow morning, the brute force of my operation will make sure I won't be dealing with them anymore."

"Casey…" Blake said aloud.

"Oh, Casey will be fine," Reegan said. "You don't have to worry about that. Casey—or as she's known here, Amy—will be relieved of the terrible memory of you, and go back into the loving arms of her husband."

"He doesn't love her," Blake said. "You know that. That's not even his *wife!*"

"He doesn't love her?" Reegan asked. He took careful steps around to Blake's left side. "Robert spent months saving to afford the costly Replicant Process for his wife. He's still paying off debt from that, some two years later. All just to see his wife again. Isn't that love?"

"He's in love with a lie," Blake said. "Same as the rest of the people you've stolen. If he knew the truth, he would have never accepted this."

"Oh, but he doesn't, does he?" Reegan said. He shined a dirty grin. "And he never will. Once HALO is taken care of, life goes back to normal for the rest of us. People will be satisfied in knowing that they can have their loved ones back. They can save those they care about from death itself. Isn't that incredible?"

"I don't understand," Blake said. "There's no way you've funded this world with the money make from this operation. You could end it. You could stop this."

"I could, sure," Reegan said. "I know I could. And you're right, I don't need this. Not anymore. But that's just the thing, Blake. I *want this.* Me and some very close friends of mine worked hard to bring this technology to life. And once I lost them, I knew I had to continue their work. For my family, if no one else. We're doing a good thing here, I promise. You just can't see the forest for the trees."

"This is wrong, Reegan," Blake shouted at the man. He knew there was no escaping this—the only thing he had control over was what he could say. He continued: "Think about the possibilities. The way our worlds could work if they were together."

"Oh, stop," Reegan said, his tone as cold as his heart. "You and I both know you don't give a damn about unity or either of the worlds. You're a selfish man, Blake. You only care about getting your wife back. And how can I blame you? I've done something rather similar."

"If you're going to erase my mind, you better do it quickly," Blake said.

"Oh, you won't lose your mind, Blake," Reegan said. "We don't erase memories. Only build upon them. We tried and tried to find a way to replace memories, but the only way to truly make someone forget something is if they remember so much else. We figured out that the mine doesn't really save, so much as rewrites itself. Whenever you recall something, it's like a painter tracing an image. It's a copy of a copy. Add enough copies, and you can change the image to something that would never resemble the original."

A flicker of hope shot through Blake. So his wife had never had her mind erased. Somewhere inside her were all her original memories. Somewhere in there was the original Casey.

"So what's next for me?" Blake asked. He wanted more information, and Reegan seemed happy to share. "Where's this world's version of me? One of your men, I presume?"

"Now you're asking the right questions," Reegan said. "But you may not like the answers you'll be getting. Because there *isn't* another you in this world."

Blake was confused—as far as he knew, this world perfectly reflected his own. Almost everyone must have had an alternate counterpart.

Which only meant that—

"Do you remember your parents, Blake?" Reegan asked. Blake's heart started to race.

This couldn't be possible...it can't be.

Images flashed in his mind. The familiarity of the town where Roger's wife had been. The rushed trip away from their home to the big city in the dead of night. The men in black that had come to tell him his parents had been killed in the streets.

"They were killed when I was young," Blake said. "Gang war. Helped me decide it would be better for me to fight that kind of evil in the world."

"But before that, Blake," Reegan asked. "What do you remember?"

This time, Reegan stepped forward with the view screen, and pulled up another image—this time, two images. The image of a husband and wife, and a small child. Blake couldn't believe it.

Those were his parents on the screen.

"They were good people," Reegan said. "They worked hard on our little cloning experiments. The problem was, they were *too good.* This whole Terminus thing was an accident. And when they found out about your world, they felt the same way you do. They wanted unity."

"You..." Blake said. "*You* sent the gang."

"I found someone I had lost in your world," Reegan said. His face showed the first genuine emotion since Blake had first seen him. "Someone I care about, *very* much. And they didn't want me to have her back. When I got her and the company, they hid from me, for longer than anyone else. Longer than you, certainly. They were becoming a problem. I had no choice."

All of the flashes of this world all rushed back to Blake. The fields that looked so familiar. The small towns, all of it...it all seemed so close to him. It *was* familiar. It was as real to him as his parents had been. He had just never known.

"There never was a gang, Blake," Reegan said. "You know that."

"Just let me have Casey," Blake said. "Just let me have my wife. We will leave. I swear to you we will disappear. We will never come back."

"That's what your parents said," Reegan said. "Before they started spreading the word about me and this place. I wanted to give them a chance. And that's a mistake I will not take twice."

The anger within Blake swelled. The same anger that he had felt in the war, with Dustin and Jordan by his side. The same anger he knew caused him to do some truly terrible things. In this moment, all Blake saw was red.

"I swear to God Reegan," Blake roared. "I will *fucking* kill you."

"Your words are useless, Blake," Reegan said. He took several steps towards the door. "You're not going to remember me, or this conversation. We'll pick a random person—one that looks just like you, or close enough to you that no one will know the difference. A person that has recently passed. We will collect their history, their searches. Their family, their friends, all the footage in the world of their existence—a digital footprint bigger than one you will ever know. We will feed this information into your mind until the name Blake Collier is as foreign as any other. And will we give you to that family, free of charge. They'll be so happy to have their loved one back, they won't even notice that you're not really them. They'll be happy, Blake. As least know you're making a family very happy today."

"Reegan!" Blake shouted at him, but he was already walking off into the darkness of the room.

"Find the closest DNA match to him," Blake could hear Reegan say to an unseen person. "Search the Cryogenic Bay. As soon as you find a close enough match, he becomes that man."

Blake could hear the door close behind him, and saw the light shut off above him.

And once again, he was in total darkness.

26

Jordan found himself in yet another holding room—this time, in what was explained to him as the base of operations for Reegan. He had been led down hallway after hallway, past wall after wall that rumbled and shook with the earth; signaling that they were clearly underground in some sort of fortress.

Jordan had been given what was explained to him as a room for 'guests of Reegan,' and his assistant make sure to emphasize how important and special it was for him to receive such a room. As for Jordan himself? He couldn't be too bothered—it was a room alike any other, and any comparison he could make was literally not from this world. He merely grunted his thanks, plopped onto the bed, and waited for future instructions.

However, those future instructions never came. It was an assistant that moved through the doors just a few hours ago, announcing simply: "Reegan has already apprehended Blake. You'll be sent back home as soon as we can. Thank you."

Before he could ask the man for further details, the assistant had left.

It was silent in the room for a long time afterwards.

It was a deafening sort of silence for Jordan, who had tried to sleep in the bed to no avail. He had been feeling more and more anxious about their current predicament ever since his encounter with Blake. The more he thought about it, the less he could understand why he was still alive. Twice Blake had the opportunity to take revenge on him, and twice he had chosen to let him live. Why? Maybe Casey had more of an effect on him after all...

But it was of little use now. Reegan had captured Blake, and soon, all would return to a relative normality for him. He would return to his own home and his own wife. He would return to his comfortable job, retire early, and think of Blake as little as possible.

But something about that possible future wasn't sitting right with Jordan. After hours of this solitude, Jordan decided push himself from the bed and open the door into the halls of Reegan's fortress.

Out here, the hallway seemed more like a hotel than a military operation—with thick carpets lining the floor and a cool, amber glow which lit the other doors in the hall. As Jordan passed these doors, he could read a few of the names of the 'honored guests,' including one *Reegan, Anne.*

So it seemed his wife was one of the visitors. Perhaps that was why this was so generous of him. Soon enough, he passed this section of the base completely, and spilled out into the concrete and steel of the main base—a more familiar sight, indeed.

He caught many stares from the other employees, who looked rather confused at the filthy and out-of-place man. He hadn't been so much as granted a shower in days. But Jordan paid them no mind, and admired the industrial architecture of the building he found himself in. The bases and headquarters on this side of the Terminus were much more technologically advanced than anything Jordan had seen or known of back home, and even though he found himself at the Ithaca base once or twice in his illustrious career, it still didn't hold a candle to the world on the other side of that Terminus.

Directions were marked on the walls, designating the clear pathways to the shuttle bays, mess hall, offices, server rooms, and other restricted areas—including ones clearly marked *Cryogenic Bay* and *Terminus*. Jordan wandered as far as he dared to go in one direction, before turning back and heading the other way. He didn't so much as want to talk to his crew, nevertheless the strangers he found himself surrounded by.

Approaching behind three men, Jordan couldn't help but listen in as he walked behind them, curious as to their conversation:

"So what's next?" one asked.

"Reegan's sending men out of Base 57 tomorrow morning," the center man said. "He's got a positive confirmation of where they're hiding out after this morning."

"I saw that earlier," the man on the right said. "You hear about how HALO had access to the satellite feeds?"

"Christ, what do you think Reegan will do to them?"

"Put them on ice with the rest of the deceased and replace them with alternates. He's not just destroying HALO—he's wiping out the memory of their existence."

The three men continued off, towards the shuttle bay, and Jordan turned away from his chase. Their conversation had left him with a sour taste in his mouth—the discussion of alternates and frozen bodies, treating those from his world like common cattle for the slaughter. Thoughts that had haunted his mind for more than a few days.

"Hey!"

The voice behind Jordan turned him quickly around to see another one of Reegan's men—this one, approaching with a bright smile and open arms. The man pulled Jordan into a hug.

"I can't believe you finally signed on!" The man beamed as the released Jordan.

"I'm sorry, I…" Jordan trailed off. *Who was this?* "You might be confused."

But the man continued to grin. "It's Riley. From recruiting? You're finally here."

"I'm sorry," Jordan repeated, feeling rather embarrassed, "I really think you have me confused with another guy. I'm not…from here."

The smile on the man's face slowly faded. "I thought you…sorry about that," he took a few steps back. "You're a spitting image of someone I used to work with. I mean, I could have sworn…"

The man seemed to stop himself, and turned away, equally as embarrassed as Jordan was.

Jordan moved quickly back through the halls and towards his room to avoid any further confusion. The more time he spent in this strange place, the less he understood what was happening. *Did that man know his alternate?* The thoughts rattled through his head as he opened the door to his room.

But before he ducked inside, he could see a tall, dark man in a business suit walking down the hall. He moved in the opposite direction—his greying hairs and abnormal height a familiar sight to Jordan, who had seen it just a few days ago.

Reegan was in the building, and unarmed.

Jordan bolted through the door before he could be seen.

More and more he was having thoughts of guilt and shame—so much so that he was even considering helping Blake again. As much as he didn't want to admit it to himself, he knew he was considering it—otherwise, he wouldn't have spent so much time analyzing the base, and the possible opportunities within it.

It wouldn't be too difficult, either. The security here seemed low and confident enough—it wasn't as if men were patrolling at all times. Knowing how strong the HALO organization was that Blake had associated him with, Jordan knew if they could just get inside, they stood a real chance.

But how would he even get them this chance? Jordan could easily escape from here, sure, but getting back inside? That was going to require a man on the inside with more than just will. It was going to require someone with biometric authentication. And he didn't even know where HALO was.

Jordan began to frantically dig around the room. Papers and fliers began to burst out into the open air and litter the floors. Jordan practically tore the bed in half as he moved to it and tossed it upwards, sending the sheets flying. He was searching for something—anything that could be of use or value in this room.

But it would be of no use. Even if he wanted to help, how could he? So much had been going through his head, he hardly knew what to think. Jordan sat for a little while afterwards in the mess he had created for himself, when a knock came at the door. Jordan lurched forward to the door and looked back to the destroyed room. He merely cracked the door open, make sure to block the view inside with his body.

Out here, Reegan's assistant seemed unhappy to see him.

"We received reports that there was a lot of noise coming from this room," the assistant said. "Is everything alright?"

Jordan's mind raced with possibilities. "Sorry, just a bit restless," he said, and looked down the hall. "Was I disturbing Reegan?"

"His wife, actually," the assistant replied. He tried to look past Jordan, but Jordan was careful to ensure that couldn't be done. "And Reegan doesn't like his wife bothered. So just...try to be a little *less* restless, if you can."

The assistant turned to leave afterwards, but Jordan wasn't done with him yet.

"One more thing," Jordan called out to the man. "A man stopped me in the hallway. He said he could have sworn he had seen me before."

"Probably your alternate," the assistant brushed off. "I wouldn't be surprised if he was a military man, like you. Hell, Roger's alternate works here, in engineering."

Jordan nodded, and closed the door.

Engineering, he thought to himself.

Maybe that was it.

***

Chamberlain arrived at the HALO hideaway a few hours afterward as planned, and most of the crew had long since fallen asleep. By the middle of the night, the only one that remained awake were the two watchmen, and Roger, who paced the outskirts of the building. Ever since Blake's arrest, he felt a great unease about him, and it wasn't just because he had been taken. Getting away from Reegan had been too simple; too easy. So to pass the time, Roger had paced circles around their hideaway in wait.

He stopped around the third or fourth pass in front of the watchmen, sitting beside them in the silence. Little more than the sound of the insects filled the air and Roger couldn't help but notice the age of the men.

These two were barely more than boys, and were now tasked with protecting not only their own lives, but the lives of everyone inside. The reality of this guerrilla war was beginning to sink into Roger. The true nature of this world, and how even though they may be much more advanced than his old world, in many ways, they seemed further behind.

"Are you from the city?" Roger asked the closer man, who turned his head towards him.

"I'm from around here, actually," he said.

"So how did you end up with these guys?"

The watchman seemed in good spirits to explain: "We're all rebellious when we're young. I guess that's never really grown out of me. I'm tired of seeing my province in the hands of selfish men. Nobody benefits but themselves."

"You don't know how many people back home would agree with you," Roger laughed. "At least some things are universal."

It felt good to have a reprise from the chaos around them, but like most things, it didn't last long. A low rumbling shook the ground, and headlights grew in brightness just off to the edge of their compound.

"Tell the others!" The watchman told Roger, and he moved with his counterpart towards the growing light.

Roger ran inside towards where Jonah, Everett, and the other men were sleeping. "Get up!" As soon as the words were spoken, a rigid military intuition kicked in, and the men were up and armed in less than a minute.

Roger returned outside to see the two watchmen surrounding a black van similar to the same one he had spent much of the past week in. The exhaust fogged the ground around them as the headlights were cut off, and flashlights mounted on the HALO rifles lit up the car.

The back doors opened, and a single man stepped out, covered head to toe in American military gear. His hands were lifted behind his back, and he walked with a wise caution.

"You better have a good reason for this, Jordan," Everett said, approaching him.

"I came to make a deal," Jordan said simply. He looked to the other men surrounding him, but not a single rifle lowered. "You're in more danger than you think."

"There's not a single good reason you could say that would get us to trust you," Everett said. His rifle was held mere inches from the Marines face, but he didn't so much as show a shred of fear.

"I know," Jordan said. "That's why I brought one."

With his words, HALO's men approached the open doors on the outside of the van. Inside, hiding in the shadows, was a moving, shaking form.

Roger approached just behind Everett, trying to ascertain what it might have been, looking closely to see in the beam of his flashlight. And as they approached, it was clear that the form was a man; tied and bound. He writhed underneath his gag and his securing ropes, and looked towards the light. And once Roger recognized the person, he took several huge steps back.

It was him.

Or rather, a version of him. A second Roger, tied and looking *very* angry in his official government uniform.

"How the hell did you get him?" Everett asked.

"One of Reegan's men let it slip that he worked in the same building I was in, so I decided to pay him a visit. Turns out, I needed someone with the right biometrics to get to your location and get out," Jordan said, then turned to Roger. "And now we have a second person with the exact biometrics to get us back in."

"You want us to help you," Everett realized.

"I can get you inside, save Blake, and stop Reegan. But we need to move. *Now*."

27

Roger soon found himself crushed up against several other bodies inside Jordan's van—his hand itching at the government uniform the was now wearing. At least it fit him well…

"We're about five minutes out," Jordan called out from the driver's seat to the others. "Get ready. They might have already noticed the van was missing."

The plan was simple—move inside the base, find Blake, and stop Reegan. But the plan was easier said than done.

HALO was outgunned and outmanned by Reegan in every possible way. They crammed every available HALO operative into the small van that they could—some twenty men. Back at HALO's hideaway, Chamberlain was mobilizing with the other men to wait with them, just outside of where Jordan had explained the facility to be. And, in the end, Chamberlain was right—it was hidden away in an old textile mill north of town, not ten miles from where HALO had been hiding away.

"We'll arrive in the vehicle bay," Jordan explained as they moved. "Once we get there, we have to move quickly. Security is low, but it isn't non-existent. It's not a matter of if we'll be caught, but when. You'll need to be in control of facility by then, or it's over."

"We'll work on that," Everett replied. He had taken up the passenger's seat. "I know my men are capable. You get Roger to Blake and find his wife. We'll work on getting into the computer mainframe. You said there was a server room?"

"I saw a sign for it, yeah."

"We'll focus on getting in there," Everett said. "We can cripple the mainframe and leak the entire system's documents onto the public internet."

"As good as that sounds," Roger said, "what's stopping Reegan from killing us all anyway?"

"We'll secure the servers, but after that, we'll do everything we can to get the rest of HALO's men inside and stopping Reegan," Jonah said. "But even if we lose the battle, if we get this information online, we win the war."

"Let's hope it doesn't come to that," Everett tried to reassure the group, but tensions were at an all-time high. This was it for HALO. Whatever happened on the other side of this night would be remembered by these men for the rest of their lives.

However long that may be.

The vehicle traveled up a dirt road, approaching what seemed to be a basic gate. When they pulled up, they could see a small scanner situated a few feet off the ground with a thumbprint scanner. It was the only way to open the gate.

Roger wiggled an arm free and moved it to the window, opening it and placing his thumb on the scanner. After a loud buzz, the gate creaked open.

"The whole province can be taken down by one building with the right thumb," Roger noted. "How foolish is that?"

"Low security means low profile," Jonah said. "We've been looking for an information hub like this for decades. Any more security like this, and we would have finally found it."

"And here we are," Everett noted.

"Here we are," Roger repeated after him.

Everett pulled the vehicle through the gate and began the descent towards the textile mill. The building here was situated deep into a natural valley in the area—obscured from being seen by the trees and tall, unkempt grass that lined the building's perimeter. The actual building itself didn't have a single exterior light—the only indication of a presence here were the beams of yellow light that shone from the old, decaying windows.

Jordan pointed Everett towards the vehicle bay—little more than a rusted garage here on the surface. The vehicle stopped outside, next to another security checkpoint. A brown box stood on a pole some three feet off the ground, and Roger was able to roll down the window to gain access.

Opening the box, a circular scanner immediately turned on, glowing the interior of the housing a dark green. Roger was able to hold his eye up to the retinal scanner, and after a moment, the garage opened.

As soon as the first light shone out from underneath the rusted metal, it was clear to Roger and the rest of the men that they were in the right place. The garage shined out a cold hue, and opened to reveal a polished concrete pathway down, into the depths of the building. Everett pulled the car inside, and descended down the pathway into a considerable vehicle bay. Underneath the surface, there must have been a complex four times the size of the textile mill that stood on the surface.

As soon as Everett parked the car, HALO's operatives exited the vehicle, and Roger was glad finally be free of the cramped car.

"There's maps of the entire complex on the view screens," Jordan explained. He moved towards a wall and removed one of the view screens from its holster. He pressed a few buttons, and activated the device.

"How did you gain access to that kind of information?" Roger asked. In response, Jordan only laughed.

"You gave it to me. Your alternate self was kind enough to give me access with enough motivation."

"How kind of me," Roger noted.

"We need to move quickly," Everett said. He moved to take one of the mounted view screens from the wall and quickly scanned the complex. He held it out for the others to see, and pointed toward one of the sections of the building. "This looks like the likely location for the server hub. If we can gain access to this room and have enough time, we can leak everything on the servers onto the public internet. That'll be the push we need to stop the trafficking once and for all."

"We're going to split off from here," Jordan cut in. "Roger and I are going to find Blake and get Casey. We're going to have to move quickly. Reegan has some sort of military outfit within a very close vicinity to this building."

"HALO is mobilizing everyone they can, but they need time," Everett said. "If we're caught or discovered too quickly, they'll mobilize and slaughter us all before HALO can come in and take the building."

Jordan nodded. "Then you'll need to shut off all communication that you can outside of this building. It won't stop Reegan from getting the word out, but it will slow him down. Every second counts."

Jonah stepped forward with several earpieces in his hand. "These are for you two, Blake, and Casey," he said to Jordan and Roger. "Keep on the same frequency. We'll be able to communicate with each other throughout the building. HALO headquarters is also on frequency. They'll be able to tell us exactly when they're ready to mobilize."

Roger placed the earpiece into his ear canal, and could almost immediately hear Chamberlain cut in: "We're moving as fast as we can. We'll need about an hour before we can move, but you need to shut down any defenses you can. If all goes well, we'll meet back up at the Terminus."

"Alright then," Everett said. He held out a hand to Jordan. "Good luck."

"Good luck," Jordan said back, shaking his hand.

Roger took one last look at HALO—the people that had protected him and saved him more than once. And suddenly, he felt a great sense of dread. An overwhelming feeling that this might be the last time he'll see these men. "I can't thank you enough," he managed to say.

"There's nothing to thank," Everett said in return. He turned from Roger, and he and the other men moved quickly out of the vehicle bay, and into the depths of the building.

***

Jordan and Roger pushed forward as quietly as they could into the depths of Reegan's base, but this was no time for caution—it was somewhere past the witching hour, and patrols of the complex seemed to be at an all-time low. The lights that shone overhead were dimmed to their lowest setting, casting dark shadows throughout the hallways and the industrial scaffolding that lay above them.

The complex was built as an intentional labyrinth for those not used to the patterns and pathways—which appeared to be one of the many defense mechanisms Reegan had implemented for his bases. The writing on the walls were helpful enough, leading the two past several offices and aisles, and towards a vague direction, labeled only 'Holding."

However, once they got close enough to see the iron door that would lead into the holding cell, they were forced to pull back, as two uniformed men exited the door. Jordan peered around the corner to see the two men standing guard in front of the door. In their hands, two rifles, armed and ready. They wouldn't stand a chance of remaining hidden if they were to take these men out by force.

Instead, Jordan's eyes turned to Roger, who was already straightening out his uniform and grasping the view screen tightly. He knew what needed to be done. Jordan held out a finger to him, signaling for him to pause. He gripped his rifle tightly, and took a few deep breaths.

Then, Jordan gave Roger the signal.

"Hey!" Roger shouted, and rounded the corner. Now distracted by the presence of another 'officer,' Jordan was able to glare around the corner undetected from the distance.

"Did somebody authorize our vehicles for dispatch?" He said to the men. Even from here, Jordan could see the confusion on the men's faces. Their rifles remained pointed to the floor, and the moved forward, towards Roger.

"What's going on?" One of the men said.

"The Shuttle Bay is empty," Roger said. He moved back towards the corner Jordan was crouched behind, drawing the two men towards him. "*I'm serious*. Nothing's in there."

The two men looked to each other, then took the bait. Both rushed forward, meeting up with Roger and following behind him as he rounded the corner.

"When did you discover this?" was the last thing the first man was able to say, before the butt of a rifle struck him square in the jaw as he moved past the corner. He fell down in a heap; his rifle clattering onto the polished floor. The second man was able to lift his rifle towards Jordan, before he too had been smashed with a rifle. Soon, two men lay on the ground, and not a single round was fired. Jordan bent down next to one of them, removing his identification card from his holster.

"Grab a body" Jordan said to Roger, lifted one of the disarmed men and moving for the iron door. Behind him, he could hear Roger following right on his heels.

The two approached the iron door next. Jordan set the body down and slid the card onto the reader next to the door. Without hesitation, the door buzzed, and opened. He lifted the body again and moved inside.

Inside, Jordan and Roger found themselves in a dark, metal hallway. The black walls and doors here were painted a crimson red from the single light above them. Jordan wasted no time in checking each door, looking inside the square opening in each, mentally marking off any which held no one.

And it seemed that all of the rooms were empty, and Jordan quickly tossed the body of the officer inside one of the rooms. Roger followed suit, and the two locked the immobilized men inside, before continuing onward. As he checked the rooms on the left, Roger checked the rooms on the right, and the two moved far down the hallway. Their search, so far, was fruitless.

That was, until Jordan opened the viewing hole on the door at the end of the hall. Inside, he could see a body strapped down to a metal table, illuminated by a single light in the darkness.

He and Roger burst through the door.

Jordan watched Blake struggle underneath the binds, but was strapped so tight, he was unable to see his rescuers from his position.

"Hey," Roger said to Jordan's left, gaining his attention. Jordan turned to see Roger in front of a small console—a single blue button glowed in the middle, clearly designated for release.

Jordan nodded, and Roger pressed the button. In the center of the room, Blake's shackles snapped open without hesitation, sending him collapsing to the floor.

Jordan rushed forward to help him up, slipping a hand underneath this arm and lifting him to his feet. "We need to move," Jordan stared. "There's not much time—"

But Blake sent a fist into his nose before he could finish the sentence.

Jordan staggered back from the blow, holding his hands to his face. By the time he felt his nose, he could already taste the iron in the blood that rushed from his nostrils. *"God!"* He spat out.

He looked up to see Blake marching towards him, ready for another fight. But this time it was Roger who interrupted them:

"Blake, stop!" Roger shouted. "We're with HALO. *All of us."*

"And just why the hell would I trust you?" Blake asked to Jordan, pain in his eyes.

"We're going to get you to Casey, and we're getting out of here."

The words were enough to stop Blake in his tracks, but froze him. He stood, panting and looking back and forth to Roger and Jordan. Finally, he spoke: "This isn't going to work," he said.

"You got any better ideas?" Jordan fired back.

It was only another ten seconds before the three of them rushed from the room. One task down, one more to go.

28

Everett led his men through the building with an ease and a confidence that only years of service had instilled in him. And why wouldn't he hold a special sort of confidence? So much of his time was spent memorizing the halls of HALO's stolen headquarters, knowing every pathway and every dead end designed by Reegan and those who had come before him. To him, this building was just another puzzle to be solved. The only struggle would be solving it without a sound.

"How are we looking on time?" He asked aloud, his finger pressed firmly on his earpiece. Chamberlain came on the other end after a good few moments of silence:

"Another forty minutes at least," she said. "We'll do our best to get you out, but remember the priority."

"I haven't forgotten," he said back to her, and continued his march.

And she was right. As much as it went against any of his own priorities, getting this information out of here was paramount to everything else—including the extraction of his own time, of Blake, or of anyone else. It wasn't hard to remember the battles and wars fought over the information that this building contained. How many sacrifices and how many good men and women had died for such a cause. And if not for that, how many had died trying to get Blake and

Roger here to give them the opportunity to do this. One of their own, Tamara, had given her own life to this cause, and she was just last in a long line to do so.

They had to get to these servers.

"How are things on your end?" Jordan's voice came his earpiece.

Everett moved in formation with the rest of his men, looking to marked signs, thinking to himself which direction Reegan was most likely to hide his key secrets. "Slowly but surely," he said. "You?"

"We've got Blake," Jordan said. "We'll have Casey soon."

Everett looked over to Jonah, who was already cracking a smile at the news. Soldier or not, he and Jonah had grown accustomed to working with Blake and Roger. To know that would end tonight either way was a bittersweet thing.

"Glad to hear it," Jonah said beside Everett, into his own microphone. "Get Casey and meet us at the rendezvous point. I'm looking forward to it."

"Over and out," came Jordan's voice, leaving the HALO operatives to continue their search of the building.

"Sir!" came another voice—this one from one of his own men. Everett turned around to see a soldier, stopped in front of one of the many doors they had passed.

Everett paced back towards his own man, looking to see what he had seen. Inside, through the glass pane, Everett could see descending stairs of concrete—out of place with the rest of the building.

"Good eye," he said to his man, pulling open the door. He and his men descended down the stairs to find themselves in utter darkness. Everett fixed a flashlight to the end of his rifle, and lifted it to shine a single column of light into their new room.

His light caught the edges of several dark towers, all humming and buzzing with life. He shined his light upwards to see an intricate tangle of wires, ascending from the towers and upwards, towards the rest of the building. "Guard the doors," he said to Jonah behind him.

They had found it.

**

Blake felt overwhelmed as he traversed the halls with Roger, and Jordan. The two hadn't really spoken since Jordan's tribunal. It was a strange feeling to be back on the same side as him—a man who had betrayed him, but had also fought beside him for years. It was as if he was wearing his old military uniform again. And he hadn't the time to cope with it.

Roger had taken the lead by this point—his eyes locked onto the view screen and the secrets it might have held. He led the group forward, past the other holding areas and towards what he had been calling a 'prison without bars.' Once the group arrived at the destination, Blake could see what he had meant.

Casey was being kept in one of the few guest rooms that Reegan had installed in the complex. Here, the walls were painted a pleasant beige color, and the polished floors turned to carpet. This specific part of the complex felt more like a hotel than a military outfit, and for good reason—it was clear that any guest needed to be kept far away from the true nature of this particular base.

"I'll be damned," Jordan said. "I was beside your wife and I didn't even know it."

"What do you mean?" Blake asked.

Jordan pointed a finger towards one of the rooms. "I was staying right here."

"Room Seven" Roger cut in, and cast a finger to his left. "Just down here. Keep quiet past Room Three. And whatever happens, don't let her scream."

"What's in room three?" Jordan asked. "Some officer?"

"No," Jordan replied. "Reegan's wife."

He needed to say no more to convince Blake to keep a low profile. This time, Roger waited at the end of the hallway, while Jordan and Blake approached Room Seven. Jordan waited for the signal from Blake, and once he nodded, opened the door with the stolen key from the soldiers back at the holding cells.

Blake cracked open the door, to see two sleeping forms on a bed in the middle of what appeared to be a rather nice hotel room. He recognized the unmistakable form of his wife under the bed, seeing her face in the light shining in from the hallway.

The two entered the room, and Jordan moved to right side of the bed, next to Casey's new 'husband.' He quickly wrapped an arm around the man's neck, sending his body into spasms.

The shaking in the bed caused Casey to stir, and her eyes opened just in time to see Blake's hand descending down on her. Within a matter of seconds, Jordan had knocked Casey's husband out cold, and Casey was stood and violently fighting against Blake, who held her against him, keeping one hand firmly over her mouth.

"Please," Blake begged into his wife's ear. "Please, stop. We're not going to hurt you." With every moment she fought against him, he wanted her to come to her senses. To see that Blake was the man she had loved, and could love again. To realize what Reegan had done to her.

But that moment never came.

"Hey," he said to her once she had exerted most of her energy. He could feel her panting against her, exhausted from the fighting. "Please, don't you recognize me?"

He had turned her around to see his face, but could only see fear in her eyes. Blake released his hand from her mouth once she seemed to stop struggling. "Please," she begged likewise. "Why are you doing this? What the hell do you want?"

"I want you to remember," Blake said. He could feel himself breaking now—looking into her eyes and seeing little more than a stranger. "I want you to know who I am."

"Chamberlain," Blake said, pushing his earpiece. "Is there nothing I can do to get her to remember?"

"We don't know," Chamberlain said. Her voice reeked of a remorse Blake never wanted to hear. "I'm sorry Blake. There's nothing we can do."

"*Blake? Blake!*" Came Roger's voice next. "There's one other thing we could try. I don't know if it'll work—"

"I don't care," Blake shot back into the earpiece, and grasped firmly at Casey's upper arm. "We'll try it." Blake looked at Casey next. "I'm sorry. You're going to have to come with us."

* * *

Jonah stood guard at the foot of the basement stairs, illuminating Everett with his flashlight. Upstairs, three of his men stood guard at the door, and were just a moment away from signaling Everett and the others to escape. Down here, every second would count.

Everett was pulling the casing off of one of the towers, some ten feet away from Jonah. Once the casing had been ripped from its position and set down on the floor, Jonah watched as Everett pulled out the virtual drive from his pocket and placed it into the terminal.

"He's just wired it in," Jonah said, his hand to his ear piece. On the other end, Chamberlain had been waiting with her best programmers to hear such news.

"We're receiving now," Chamberlain confirmed. "We'll need a minute to finish the download on this end."

"It's going to come in encrypted," Everett said. He had taken a step back and was looking up and down the room, and at the dark towers that lined the halls. "All of it will."

199

"As long as we have it, it's only a matter of time," Chamberlain said on the other end. "Nothing is full proof. Are you sure this is the correct tower?"

"They're all the right tower," Jonah clarified. "The system is linked linearly, like a daisy chain. Access one, and you access them all."

"Simple enough," came Chamberlain's response, leaving the two back to their work. And soon enough, quiet returned to the room as the only noise that came from around them were the gentle hums of fans, milling away at their work within the towers…

Until a loud crash rang out from the far corner of the room.

Jonah's eyes narrowed and looked directly towards Everett. His hands grasped his rifle even tighter, and he slowly raised it at the ready.

Everett's gaze darted towards the noise, and then back to Jonah. From what it seemed, something, or someone, was still in this room, several rows away from them. Everett lifted a finger first to Jonah, then to the source of the noise.

This was his job, and his alone to handle.

Jonah took several careful steps away from Everett, losing sight of him in the grid of server towers. In a room as sensitive as this, firing even a single direct round would be too risky. A stray bullet could wipe out any data Everett was harvesting for HALO, and certainly alert Reegan of their intrusion. Leaving the threat was not an option either.

And so, Jonah took the only step he could. He closed his eyes, lifted a hand to the front of his rifle, and switched off his light, sending himself into the darkness of the room.

When he opened his eyes, faint green dots were all that he could make out—lit markings on the towers to indicate their status. Using these as a guide, he began to pace forward, slipping the rifle onto his back. His free hands now lifted upward—ready for combat of any sort.

"We need another few minutes," came Everett's voice into his earpiece. He spoke in a hushed whisper. "We can't stop. Not now."

Slowly but surely, he approached the source of the noise. The corner of the room here held a fewer number of towers than the center that they had arrived in—the green lights that served as his path forward were beginning to grow less and less common. The buzzing fans that had hid his breath were fading away, and soon enough, his own sharp breaths were the only sound he could hear.

In and out. In and out.

Until he felt a sharp force smash into his side, and he toppled to the floor.

Without the ability to see, Jonah's senses were knocked into overdrive—every fiber of his being trying to discern which way was up and which way was down. He felt a sharp pain eat at his left side, and a large body on top of him. It was another half second before he realized he was pinned to the ground, and felt strong hands wrap around his neck.

Jonah wrestled his right hand free from underneath his attacker's knee, and sent a fist upwards in the dark. He felt himself make contact, and felt the body shift and buckle from the strike. Using this as leverage, Jonah pushed upwards and outward, shifting the attacker off of his body. He swung his arms wildly together in the air, grasping at the body. And once he found what seemed to be the neck, he quickly wrapped an arm around it, holding his inner elbow against the man's Adam's apple.

Within ten seconds, he felt the body go limp, and released.

"Jonah?" He heard Everett's voice call out. "*Jonah!*"

"He's down," Jonah panted. His hands were on his back now, searching for his rifle and flashlight. "Did we get it?"

"We got it," Everett called back. Even from here, Jonah could hear the relief in his voice.

"We have it."

***

Roger had been leading Blake and the others through another long series of halls, being careful to avoid what he called "the main arteries of the base." He kept his nose down in his view screen, moving several paces in front of Blake, Casey, and Jordan, who tailed behind at the ready.

"Roger, please," Blake said, rushing to catch up to him. "Where are we going?"

But Roger didn't answer the question. Instead, he rushed around yet another corner. And once Blake had followed around, he could see two thick, kitchen-like doors at the end of this hall. Above it, the sign read: *Cryogenic Bay - CLIMATE CONTROLLED.*

"If anything will work," Roger finally answered, "it might be this."

Blake watched as Roger pushed open the doors, allowing the freezing air to flow out into the hallway and rush past. He turned around to see Casey, still scared and confused, look to him, then back towards the doors. Behind her, Jordan stood guard, and waited.

Casey was first to move on her own accord— following Roger through the doors. But why? There was no reason for her do to this…not unless she thought there was something worthwhile inside. Could she remember again? Just the idea gave Blake enough hope to follow close behind her, through the doors, and into the Cryogenic Bay.

In here, the air opened up, and their footsteps reverberated throughout the room. Once Roger had flipped the switch to the lights, rows of overhead cut on above them, staggering and revealing the massive room they found themselves in. Rows upon rows of silver cabinets stretched what seemed to be hundreds of feet down and away from them. This place must be nearly half of the square footage of the rest of the building that he had seen.

"What's your name?" Roger asked towards Casey.

She spoke next with a hesitant tone, as if she were asking a question: "Amy Webb," she said.

Roger looked down to the view screen and pushed a few buttons. Clearly, from his time in the HALO archives, he had learned a thing or two. He looked up soon after, and locked eyes with her again: "Follow me."

Roger led Casey and Blake about fifty feet inside the room, down one of the many hallways. Here, Blake could see the rows and rows of drawers above him, lining the aisles from the floor to near fifteen feet above his head. These were marked solely with six-digit numbers, and were indistinguishable. The organization alone must have cost a fortune to conjure up.

"Reegan seems to keep exhaustive records," Roger said as they walked. But Blake had a sneaking suspicion he understood what was going on here. Still, he listened to Roger: "Both digital and physical records. Each one of these drawers align with a name in a database. The number of drawers here are ten times the names on the registry, so he must have been planning some sort of aggressive expansion."

He stopped suddenly in his tracks, in front of a drawer about waist high to his left. "I don't know what you're going to find in here, Amy," he started, "but…this is your drawer."

Blake kept his distance. He had spent enough time in a mortuary to know what may lie inside the drawer. "Why would he keep these?" He asked.

"Paranoia, safe-keeping…I can't be sure," Roger said. "Maybe to match the visuals of one person to the next. Maybe to prevent HALO from digging up proof of Reegan's crimes from the graves."

Blake watched as Casey pulled on the drawer, which opened with a thick hiss and a puff of slow-moving fog, which raised slightly into the air, before pouring back down onto the floor beneath them. The drawer opened six feet outward automatically, and once the dust began to settle, Blake could make out an unmistakable silhouette.

Even if he knew it wasn't his wife—even if he knew the person in that drawer wasn't the woman he loved, he couldn't stand to look at her like this. Blake turned away, putting an arm against the wall and leaning his face into it. *What was the point of all of this?* The Casey he knew might not be recoverable. Surely Reegan tried to stop him from seeing her, in the hopes that he could bring her memories back, but even that had failed. What use was it to traumatize this woman any further with kidnapping, and forcing her to see her own former self, laying as a corpse in a morgue?

The room around them was silent, and out of the corner of his eye, he could see Casey lower herself towards the form in the drawer. Before he could see any more, he took a few steps away, towards the door. Overwhelmed in the moment, he finally, briefly considered that he may never see Casey again. Not the real Casey.

Not the woman he loved, but just a shadow of the woman she used to be.

Until, behind him, in a small and worried voice, he heard Casey speak:

"Blake?"

The single word—just his name alone, was spoken in a manner he hadn't heard in years. He swiftly turned around, to see a new set of eyes in Casey.

The eyes of his wife.

"Blake?" she asked again, tears forming in her eyes.

The two rushed to each other, and embraced once again, for the very first time.

29

One the data had cleared, there wasn't a second to be wasted.

HALO confirmed over the communication channel that they had received all they could from the servers underground—all in one encrypted file. They would need to spend hundreds of man hours trying to pry open its digital lock, but now, greater threats remained.

Everett gathered up his team after Jonah had taken out the last remaining guard in the server room. He was successful, with a small caveat—the attacker had managed to slice deep into Jonah's left side. He moved with a considerable strain up the concrete steps and back out into the halls.

"We've cleared the data on our end," Everett said into his ear piece. "We're moving for the Terminus now."

Next came Roger's voice on the line, relaxed and loose: "Copy that. We're having a bit of a reunion here. We'll be up with Casey shortly."

"Congratulations, Blake," Everett said next. "There'll be time for celebration on the other side. For now, let's get you home."

Everett led his men back through the wiry halls of the underground complex. They moved with a purpose and with fully attuned eyes, but were becoming more and more surprised by the lack of guards. The process to receive the data had been easy...perhaps too easy. But if he was able to get his men to the Terminus, they could meet up with Blake, Casey, Roger, and Jordan, and get them home within a day using HALO's combined knowledge. In a fortnight, Reegan could be taken down. And all of the sacrifices his men had to make might have been worth it.

The men ascended several flights of stairs to find themselves in a final stretch of hallway. Here, mirrors lined the walls, directing them forward towards the final set of doors. On them, *Terminus* was inscribed in bold, silver lettering.

The men pushed forward, opening the doors.

Inside, Everett found himself looking upwards. Here, the exterior of the building comprised of the ceiling and walls—the entire holding area for the Terminus was actually in the hollowed out center of the former textile mill. Broken glass shards and debris lined the perimeter of the open space, but soon cleared towards the center, as scaffolding and staircases led directly upward towards the center of the room, where the Terminus could easily be seen. Everett quickly estimated the room to be nearly a baseball field in size and scope, and its center platform rose nearly three stories in the air. From their vantage point, they couldn't see what lay on top of the platform—only the tall, sinister Terminus.

But they did hear the voice of Reegan, the moment it called out from the top of the platform:

"You didn't think you'd actually get away with this, did you?"

As Everett's heart sank, Reegan and severed armed guards walked towards the edge of the raised platform, and into view of Everett and Reegan's men. Behind them, he could hear the doors inside of the Terminus lock shut automatically.

They were trapped.

"You were smart enough to use Roger to enter, sure," Reegan continued, "but you didn't possibly think I'd leave myself so vulnerable, so...unprotected. You were spotted in a moment. The second you stepped into my halls I've been watching you."

"What does it matter?" Everett asked. He looked to his men, who were already preparing for a war. "We've taken your information. HALO has everything you've hidden away here. Within a day every cruel thing you've ever done will be online for all the world to see."

"Sir, you underestimate me," Reegan replied. "I wouldn't just leave my most precious secrets out in some server room, for the nearest mine with a virtual drive to access. You retrieved dummy files. Empty binary code. You weren't even smart enough block the virtual address you were sending your files to." Reegan lifted the view screen that had been in his hands. "Thanks to you, we were able to pinpoint the exact location of the rest of your little army. A concentrated strike force just a button push away from turning the rest of HALO to *ash*. But first, I have one last issue to take care of."

Everett turned to Jonah and the rest of his men, but could only see a single emotion on their faces—loss.

Reegan had bested them in every possible way—he had allowed them the illusion of sneaking into his base, and stealing his information, when in reality, they had given him what he wanted. He now had Blake and Roger, the defected Jordan, and the precise location of HALO. And, he held his finger on the trigger to end all three.

"You fought a good fight, Officer," Reegan said, "but you've lost." He turned next to one of his armed men, before moving back out of sight. As he did, Everett distinctly heard him say: "We're done here."

And with that, a sea of bullets rained down from the platform above, directly onto HALO's men below.

"Hit the deck!" Everett screamed. His eyes scanned for the first sign of cover—a few upturned pieces of concrete left over no doubt from the destruction of the textile mill. He felt a sharp bite in his right leg just above the calf, and collapsed onto the floor just as he had arrived at the concrete. Dust and dirt was flying in the air all around him, and chipped away at his makeshift cover almost immediately. Flying colors of neon from the tracer rounds lit the room in a terrible haze. He slammed his back into the concrete, and looked back to his right.

Three of his man lay motionless where they had once stood. Several others had taken refuge behind similar abandoned hunks of scaffolding and shrapnel. Alongside him, he could see that Jonah had followed his lead, and remained pushed up against the same wall as him.

He lowered a gloved hand onto his calf, but couldn't cope with the pain of touching it. Blood oozed from the bullet wound and dripped onto the dirt below.

Everett swung his rifle around in the air, positioning it on top of the concrete mound. He lifted his head for a fraction of a second, fired four controlled rounds, and ducked back under cover, just as a flurry of bullets had been sent his way. A second later, the familiar thud of a body could be heard over the gunfire. He glanced over to the base of the platform to see his target on the floor—having fallen from the platform after receiving three rounds to the chest.

There was fight in him yet.

***

Blake's ecstasy was cut short by a terrible ringing in his ear piece. After Casey had finally recognized him, he and her had been embracing ever since. What was only a minute at most felt like a lifetime to him. He wanted nothing more than to hold her here, and apologize. For every misguided action he had ever taken. For not being able to protect her until it was too late.

But the world couldn't spare a moment.

"We're under attack!" Everett shouted over the communications link. In the background, gunfire could be heard. "Reegan knew we were here! We're being amused!"

Blake tried to get a hold of his senses, and turned to see Roger, who was already running far from the aisle and towards the exit of the Cryogenic Bay.

"What..what's going on?" Casey asked, her hands still wrapped around his arms. She was confused and overwhelmed with the revelation she had just gone under. "I don't...I don't know where we are."

"We have to move," Blake tried to explain. He grabbed her hand and began to jog towards the exit, behind Roger. Casey followed with much hesitation, so he continued: "We have to get out of here, and the people that are trying to help us are under attack."

Casey's eyes seemed to narrow, and she lifted her free hand from her side to her temples as she moved alongside him. "I remember the names...I think...Reegan United, HALO...it's all in there."

"HALO brought me to you," Blake explained. The two pushed out of the Cryogenic Bay to find Roger already with Jordan.

"Jordan?" Casey asked. Blake watched as Jordan and Casey tried make sense of it all.

"A lot has happened," Blake said, "and I can explain later. But we need to help them, or they're going to die."

Needing no further push, Jordan began to take off towards the Terminus, and Roger, Blake, and Casey all pushed forward with him. Now finally together, the entourage rushed through the empty halls, following the marking on the wall that pointed them towards the Terminus.

As they reached the stairs upwards, however, shots were quick to fire from the top of the staircase. Jordan and the others ducked out of the way of the shots, as more of Reegan's men stood guard of the Terminus.

Blake, Casey, and Roger stayed far back, ducked around a corner and out of the line of fire. From his vantage point, Blake could see Jordan lean out and return fire, before returning to cover.

"They're trying to stop us from getting to the Terminus!" Jordan shouted towards Blake. "If we don't get in there quickly, everyone from HALO is going to die."

Chamberlain was next to come on the channel. "We need more time! We're on the way, but you're miles from our location. We're moving as fast as we can."

Next, Everett chimed in, cluttering the feed with the sounds of gunfire: "You don't have time! Reegan tricked us. If we don't stop him, it's over for the convoy, and it's over for HALO. You need to burn back!"

"It's now or never, Everett," said Chamberlain. "We're not turning around. Stop Reegan and we'll get you out of there."

"There has to be something we can do," Roger said. He looked to Blake with a worried expression. "Me and Casey can't fire a gun. We're no use to Jordan and them."

"I can scare them from coming down," Jordan said, "but I can't stop them. They have the high ground!" And indeed, he was right. Jordan was essentially taking pot shots upwards towards an unseen enemy, who was using the same strategy to attack back. They were in a stalemate—exactly what Reegan would want. They couldn't arrive at the platform in time to stop the slaughter of HALO soldiers—even if they couldn't it wouldn't be enough. And in five minutes, all of HALO itself gets blown sky high. Reegan would win.

They needed a Hail Mary, and fast. And Blake knew exactly what could work.

"Roger, Casey," Blake said after a moment of epiphany. "With me."

Casey and Roger nodded, and Blake took off without a moment to spare—back into the depths of the military compound.

"Where are you going?!" Blake could hear Jordan shouting at him, but he never stopped his pace.

"Everyone," he said into his ear piece, "hold out as long as you can. We're going to play the only card we have."

If this wasn't going to work, nothing ever would.

***

Back at the Terminus, a massacre was unfolding.

Everett and his men were doing the best they could to fight back against the raining rounds against them, but Reegan's men had an advantage they did not. On top of the platform, a few steps back would protect them again any rounds fired from HALO. But the other way around, Reegan's men were shooting at them like fish in a barrel.

"We need ground!" Jonah called out to Everett. In the fray, he had moved up a few feet closer to the staircase to the top of the platform. "If I could get enough cover to get to these stairs, we might have a chance!"

"We have to keep them occupied!" Everett called back. "We need to buy as much time as we can!"

The skeptic in him knew the futility of the situation. Everett and the other men knew nothing about where Blake had run off to. If he was a smart man, he, Casey, and Roger were escaping in the madness that was unfolding. But even if he was trying to stop Reegan, what was there left to do? In a moment, Chamberlain and the rest of HALO would be wiped from the face of the earth. It was only minutes after that when an entourage of Reegan's men would surely march in and wipe them out.

Everett looked to see his other men, only to bear witness to an ever-growing body count. Four more of his men were strewn across the makeshift battlefield—their chests stained the same crimson red color that poured the life from their bodies. His men looked to him with fear and

211

trepidation—without a guide and a strategy, they were hopeless against Reegan's attacks.

This was their last stand. And if it was truly to be the end, Everett was not going to let it end cowering beneath a pile of concrete.

Everett let out a pained yell as he lifted himself to his feet, feeling the bullet lodged in him strain under his own weight. He rushed forward to Jonah's position, taking another bullet in the shoulder as he did so. He collapsed nearly on top of his friend, and quickly tried to regain his composure.

The two men looked to each other now in a mutual calm. This was the moment they had been preparing for. And after all of their hard-fought battles, maybe it was fitting to make the last stand here—in the heart of Reegan's home.

"We got pretty far, didn't we?" Everett nearly laughed aloud. His bright smile was soon spread across Jonah's own face.

"Yeah," Jonah said. "We did."

"On the count of three," Everett said, "we charge for the staircase. Let's see how many of these guys we can take out."

Jonah nodded. "Let's do it."

Everett forced himself into a crouched position, and lifted his eyes above cover to gain a visual of the staircase. From here, it was only twenty feet away. If they charged it, who knows? Maybe they'd take down enough men with them to make some sort of difference. He allowed himself to look back to his friend, one last time.

"One…"

"Two…"

"*Stop!*"

A voice shouted from the doors of the Terminus, so loud and so forceful, even Reegan's men held fire long enough to see who the source was.

Standing in the doorway, several of Reegan's men, now unarmed, stood in the doorway. Behind them, Everett could make out Jordan—his rifle armed at the men's backs.

And standing in the center of it all was Blake. Standing tall and fearless, looking to the top of the platform.

And sure enough, Reegan did humor him. Everett could see Reegan's form once again approach the edge of the platform, his hands clearly holding the view screen tightly. He was just a push away from dropping hellfire down on HALO, but even now, took the time to engage: "And what is this?"

"Call off the airstrike on HALO," Blake replied. "*Now.*"

"And why would I do that?"

With his words, it was as if the red sea itself had parted between Reegan's captive men. Standing in the center of them, Roger and Casey took a few steps forward, entering the room.

And between them, stood a disheveled, tired, and heartbroken Anne Reegan.

"Jon," she asked. "Is it true?"

The room was silent for several seconds, before Everett could see Reegan give a wave to his soldiers and move for the staircase. "Hold your fire!" he shouted to them. "Lower your rifles, for God's sake!"

Reegan quickly descended downward and crossed the war-torn pathway from the foot of the stairs towards the entrance of the room. Here, Everett could see him slow down—his pace becoming more and more hesitant as he approached his wife. "Anne," Reegan said, his voice quivering. "Are you okay? Did they do anything to you?"

But Anne's face showed anything but fear. Her glare contorted to a pained shock. Everett could see tears forming in her eyes. "Tell me they're lying Jon. I need you to tell me they're lying."

***

213

Blake wasn't lying to Anne. He had remembered something Reegan had said, something so quick and so honest, Reegan probably didn't even remember saying it as he gloated in his victory over Blake.

I've done something rather similar.

Five short words which had implicated the world to Blake. Reegan wasn't some foul monster, running amok and stealing because of some skewed perception of joy. No, he was more human than that. Reegan must have been working simply to bring his wife home to him. The same wife that stood in front of him now, convinced of the greater truth—that she, like Casey, had been stolen from another world, another far from here. Blake's parents must have tried to stop him, and paid with their lives.

And all it had taken to create a crack in the hull of Reegan's lies to her was to tell her the story of themselves. To come to her room and show her the name *Amy Webb* in the computer system, next to another name: *Casey Collier.* And hundreds of other names—lives stolen from other worlds, in a grand conspiracy that she had ever known of.

Blake and Casey had explained their story together to her and created enough doubt in her mind to have her come with them, forcing Reegan's men to stand down or murder their leader's wife. And here they were, confronting Reegan with his one and only real weakness.

The truth.

Something stronger than any machine could steal from the mind of Anne Reegan, or the woman she was before this. No matter how much Reegan had tried to erase the past, he never really could, could he? He could only change the future.

And today, that was coming to an end.

"I don't know what you're talking about," Reegan said to her. "I don't know what they've told you."

But Anne could clearly see through the facade now. Blake watched as Reegan took another step forward, only for

Anne to take another step back. "I remember another life," she said. "Another family. I don't understand."

"They're feeding you lies, Anne," Reegan was beginning to plead. "They're showing you things that aren't even *real*. I know you, I know you know the truth—"

"The truth?" Anne asked. "I never knew about this place." She pointed upwards to the platform. "This...this *thing* you've constructed. I always thought HALO was fighting against you...but they're fighting against what you've *done*."

Blake could see the heartbreak in Reegan's eyes. "Anne," he said. "Please—"

"Call off the airstrike, Jon," Anne interrupted. "No one else needs to die because of you."

Reegan paused in place, looking to no one other than Anne. It was as if the world had faded from his sight—neither Blake nor Casey and Roger, either HALO's army or his stood in the room right now. Only husband and wife. And Blake knew that in that moment, that's all that really mattered. The empire that he had created failed at its original purpose; returning Reegan's wife to him.

Blake could almost feel bad for him.

Reegan lifted the view screen to his view and pressed a button on the screen, before throwing it to his side. The tempered glass shattered onto the dirt floor.

"You are my wife," Reegan said. "You have been my wife for more than thirty years."

"No, Jon," came Anne. *"Someone else was."*

Soon after, the glass windows of the great facade around them—the old textile mill that had served as cover for Reegan and his empire—shattered and gave way to the entering HALO force. Scores and scores of new soldiers ambushed the exterior of the textile mill, pouring into the room in overwhelming numbers. The entire HALO strike force in the region had been gathered, and were now descending upon the building. Outside, Blake could hear the roar of armored trucks and the marching of more men.

He gave the signal to Jordan, who stepped forward with a pair of handcuffs, and moved to Reegan. Reegan didn't fight, or flee. Instead, he stood motionless as Jordan handcuffed him, keeping eyes only on Anne.

In front of them, on the platform, HALO operatives rushed the staircase and soon ascended towards the last of Reegan's men. Each threw down their arms, and quickly surrendered.

To his right, he would feel a gentle hand wrapping around his own. And as he looked to his side, he could see Casey, tired and weary from the journey, exhausted and confused with the world around her...

But he saw his wife again. He could see the light of the woman he loved in those eyes. And so he pulled her to him, and pressed his lips onto hers.

And so ended the reign of Reegan United.

30

From the ashes of Reegan United, a new world had to rise. Such a task would take longer than any one mission or battle.

After the attack on Reegan's base, HALO quickly unleashed the sum total of the information hidden throughout his multiple caches and complexes. As a prisoner of war now, Reegan was surprisingly helpful—every password and encrypted file was provided without issue or argument. He had played the game, and he had lost. There was no room for pride in those who lose.

Families were torn apart the day the information was released. Fathers who had discovered that their sons were from another world. Wives with false husbands. Children with false mothers. The implication of the truth rocked the world far and wide, and in the vacuum of leadership, HALO struggled to keep the peace. Quickly, the world was fractured into factions about what to do, who to elect, and what crimes could be charged against the men and women who had served under Reegan—especially who had known of the atrocities committed. A coalition was being assembled now. One to answer the trying questions of a lost world.

Blake saw little of Chamberlain and Everett after that day. Both had gone to the central district to try and keep a level of decorum for HALO. And they faced more than the fear and apprehension of an empty office in the highest level of power. Now, with their task complete, even those in HALO began to disagree with each other to some extent. The road to democracy for a world that knew little of it wasn't simple, nor were the answers as clear-cut or as noble as anyone was hoping or expecting. In fact, it was Roger who had taken the reigns to help out. His knowledge of both this world and the last made him an unlikely diplomat to HALO operatives.

As for himself and for Casey, Blake had chosen to remain inside the military complex for much of the transitional period. The days passed quickly as he and Casey remained in their room, picking up with themselves where they had left off. They spoke to each other as if they had been old friends rather than lovers—and began to rekindle their lost relationship.

Casey spoke positively of much of this world—as a side-effect of the memory alterations, she retained parts of the life of the woman she had inhabited for two years. She could recall with a warmth both life in the town home here, as well as her life back in New York. As for Robert, her false husband, she had spoken to him at length to try to give the man some sort of closure on his own loss. He left a few days later with the body of his former wife, wanting to ensure it received a proper funeral. And no matter how hard Blake wanted to hate him for stealing Casey away from him, the truth was, he had just been another victim of the world Reegan had created.

As for Jordan, it was lovely to finally get some sense of closure from the events that had separated Blake from his former friend. He and Jordan spent a fair amount of time recalling their former lives in Afghanistan, and the men they used to be. They even received closure on the issue of Dustin—Reegan had admitted the man had never been killed in case he proved to be useful, and HALO transferred him to the complex about a week after the collapse of Reegan

United. Blake and Dustin spent a large amount of time with Jordan, reconciling their differences, and nursing their wounds in battle. For they were older men now, and all of them hoped that they had served their final days in the service of others. Jordan and Dustin both talked of retiring as soon as they returned stateside, as to hopefully rebuild another life in the same way Blake had.

And they were given the opportunity soon. The Terminus was damaged in battle, but became operational once again nearly two weeks later. HALO engineers and Reegan United engineers worked side-by-side to uncover the mystery of the design, and turn it on for what seemed to be one of the final times. The politics in the central district seemed to be leaning towards decommissioning all connections with the other world, in the hopes of sparing any others from suffering from that kind of power.

And so the morning after the Terminus was operational, Jordan and Dustin bid their goodbyes to Roger and Blake. They hoped the see them well on the other side as soon as they were ready to leave, and promised Blake and Casey specifically that they would work to recover some semblance of a relationship with them. Blake felt happy for his former men as they moved forward and disappeared into the Terminus in a brilliant flash of light.

Blake, Casey, and Roger scheduled their own departure a few days later, in order to say their goodbyes in a proper fashion. Blake and Everett shared a final meal together, before Everett was off to return to the business in the central district. He wished Blake safe travels and a happy marriage, before leaving entirely. Chamberlain herself was unable to leave the district for a personal goodbye, but shared a friendly phone conversation between Blake and Casey, hoping the best for them all in the other world. Jonah was kind enough to present Blake, Casey, and Roger each with a small token of HALO's appreciation—a military decoration for the each of them, as a reward for their service to their world. Blake promised Jonah he would cherish it always, before seeing him off to service in the southeast district, and his former home before joining the war effort.

The morning came at last, and Blake, Casey, and Roger ate a final meal together in the cafeteria—away from the remaining HALO men. Now that their friends had left them, the true reality was beginning to set in; they were visitors in this world, and their welcome was beginning to be overstayed.

After breakfast, the three packed their bags of what little they had brought with them, and moved up the flight of stairs, down the mirrored hallway, and into the main room of the Terminus. They ascended the staircase, and stood in position as instructed by the engineers.

But something was off about Roger. He had moved to the Terminus with a certain hesitation in his pace. Breakfast had been quieter for usual for him, and Blake had noticed his distance during the past several days. At first, he had figured it was about leaving behind a world he had come to enjoy, more so than Blake had. Or perhaps it was the reality that he had come this far, only to leave his sister behind. He never spoke of her. Not anymore.

But as he stood on the platform next to Blake and Casey, he finally spoke up:

"Blake," Roger started, "I don't think I'll be coming with you."

A part of Blake had really known this moment was coming, but hearing the words aloud was enough to shock him with the reality of the statement. This might be the final time he would see his friend. "Roger—"

"I don't want to argue with you, Blake," Roger said. His eyes showed a sadness even as he forced a smile for his friend. "I just don't think there's much back there for me to return to. You have home with you. And I think there's still time for me to build a new home here."

"You've always got a home with us, Roger," Casey said. She and Roger had grown close these past few weeks.

"Thank you," Roger said. "You'll look after Blake, won't you?"

Casey nodded, and stepped forward. The two embraced for a short while, before Roger released her, and turned to Blake.

"I can help HALO here," Roger explained. "I can make a real difference. I can make sure what happened to you and me will never happen again."

"I understand," Blake admitted. "I just don't want to see you go."

Blake moved forward out of instinct, embracing his friend. Over these past few weeks, he and Roger had been through hell and back together. And if this was the last time he would see him, he wanted him to know that his friendship and his loyalty had meant the world to him. Even when everyone else had left.

Once the two released each other, Roger seemed almost tearful as he moved from the platform: "*Godspeed, you two.*"

"Thank you, Roger," Blake called back to his friend. "For more than you know."

The sadness of Roger's decision to stay soon faded, as he felt Casey grasp the hand at his side. The two looked to each other first for a long moment, before turning their attention forward, to the Terminus just ten feet ahead of them.

"Auxiliary power, check," the engineers said at the machine's control. "Gateway control, check. All systems operational. Clear for dispatch."

The walls of the hollow circle began to glow a familiar red, then white, then a brilliant blue, as the Terminus filled with life and light. Thick bands of wind escaped from the center of the Terminus, blowing so fiercely and quickly, Blake and Casey were nearly knocked off of their feet.

The head engineer gave the signal for the two of them—it was time to leave.

Blake and Casey stepped forward, hand in hand, and approached the machine. Blake took one last look to his left to see Roger—the winds blowing stray strands of hair against his face.

He looked truly happy.

Satisfied, he and Casey approached the vortex ahead, together at last.

The winds soon gave way. The pushing forces upon their bodies suddenly pulled them into the Terminus, and Blake's vision was filled with a brilliant flash of white light.

And then, they were home.

THE END

EPILOGUE

The D.C. Metro was much simpler than the Subway back home.

The system had been organized into several distinct colored lines, as opposed to New York's more complex array of colors, numbers, and names. It made life much simpler for Blake, who had flown to the airport and hopped right onto the correct subway line without so much as stepping outside.

In here, the familiar tight corridors of New York's system were replaced by large, grid-like arches that made up each stop. Blake could imagine the level of traffic that moved in and out of here on a regular day—the immigration of hundreds of government employees into and out of the White House. The thought alone made Blake wonder which faces in the crowd had known about the truth. Which faces were hiding more than they showed.

But, that was not why Blake was here—and he certainly wasn't around during peak hours. In fact, it was a Thursday night, and Blake found himself practically alone in the Farragut North stop, and within the hour, the Metro would be closed altogether.

Blake looked down to his watch, and noted that it was just a few minutes before 11:30 at night. At 11:31, the last train to the rail's terminus at Glenmont would depart, and Blake would likely be asked to leave.

Impatient at the wait, Blake pulled his phone from his pocket and flipped through the past few messages. He had double-checked with Jordan to see if his information about today was correct, and as of a few hours ago, his target should still be arriving any moment. And hopefully so. Spending too much time apart from home and from Casey reminded him of darker times. Times he'd sooner forget, if he received the closure he hoped to tonight. He hated to leave her alone to pack their things as they prepared to move from the city.

Then, on the other side of the tracks, he spotted him—a dark figure, wrapped tightly in a pea coat, shivering from the cold above ground. The man took careful steps down into the main station, and kept a glare towards the floor.

Blake rose from his seat and approached the edge of the track. From here, he could feel the faint rumble in the concrete beneath him. And to his left, florescent lights glowed in the tunnel that would bring about this man's departure from the city.

Blake leaned forward, trying to ascertain a good look of him. The man kept a low glare, now to his phone, and didn't so much as flinch as the train pulled into the station. The train blocked the man's view from Blake momentarily, before Blake could once again see him through the stationary windows.

Blake paced several feet along the edge of the tracks to get a clear sight of the man as he entered the train by himself. He took a seat, leaned his head back against the headrest, and took in a deep breath. Which was all Blake needed to see.

Inside the train car, the man rubbed at his eyes and tried to fight the cold and the sleep as they took him. Today had been a long day at work for him, and tomorrow would prove to be even longer.

But something rather peculiar caught his eye. Outside the train window, just to the right and alongside the tracks, a man stood alone—watching him. He stood with a firmness and kept his hands in his pockets, but moved away as soon as the two made eye contact.

And as the train rolled away from the station and took him home, the man would wonder if he had really seen anyone that at all on the other side of the tracks, or if it had all been inside of his head.

Because he could have sworn he saw himself.

ABOUT THE AUTHOR

Jason Yormark is a 20 year marketing and blogging veteran having written for multiple publications and websites over the years. Originally from the northwest suburbs of Chicagoland, Jason moved to the Seattle area and now calls Monroe, WA his home with his wife Molly and two boys Jacob and Justin. MIRRORS is Jason's first novel to be published with many more to come. To learn more about Jason, the MIRRORS journey and future projects, visit www.jasonyormark.com.